THE SECRET SPIRAL

Also by Gillian Neimark

The Golden Rectangle

The Secret Spiral

Gillian Neimark

ALADDIN

New York London Toronto Sydney New Delhi

ALADDIN

An imprint of Simon & Schuster Children's Publishing Division
1230 Avenue of the Americas, New York, NY 10020
First Aladdin paperback edition January 2013
Copyright © 2011 by Jill Neimark
All rights reserved, including the right of reproduction in whole or in part in any form.
ALADDIN is a trademark of Simon & Schuster, Inc., and related logo is a registered trademark of Simon & Schuster, Inc.
Also available in an Aladdin hardcover edition.
For information about special discounts for bulk purchases, please contact Simon & Schuster Special Sales at 1-866-506-1949 or business@simonandschuster.com.
The Simon & Schuster Speakers Bureau can bring authors to your live event.
For more information or to book an event contact the Simon & Schuster Speakers Bureau at 1-866-248-3049 or visit our website at www.simonspeakers.com.
Designed by Lisa Vega
The text of this book was set in Manticore.
Manufactured in the United States of America 1212 OFF
2 4 6 8 10 9 7 5 3 1
The Library of Congress has cataloged the hardcover edition as follows:
Neimark, Gillian.
The secret spiral / by Gillian Neimark. — 1st Aladdin hardcover ed.
p. cm.
Summary: Chef and wizard Dr. Pi, owner of the Sky-High Pie Shop, tries to persuade ten-year-old Flor Bernoulli to accept her destiny as the next important member of a historic family of mathematicians.
ISBN 978-1-4169-8040-7 (hc)
[1. Mathematics—Fiction. 2. Space and time—Fiction.
3. Pies—Fiction. 4. Fantasy—Fiction.] I. Title.
PZ7.N42945Se 2011
[Fic]—dc22
2010020974
ISBN 978-1-4169-8041-4 (pbk)
ISBN 978-1-4169-8526-6 (eBook)

For Kelly Connor

If you haven't found something strange during the day,

it hasn't been much of a day.

—JOHN ARCHIBALD WHEELER

CONTENTS

Chapter 1

INTRODUCING FLOR THE PIE GIRL, DR. PI, AND MRS. PLUMP

It was a Wednesday in May when Flor's life changed forever. That was when the world she knew collapsed—her familiar, ho-hum, humdrum, oh-so-comfy world in Brooklyn Heights, New York, in the rooftop apartment she shared with a proud white cat named Libenits and her mother, a fashion photographer. That was the day she learned that life was way wackier than anyone could ever have guessed. That was the time she peeked around the curve of time itself, and a hat took her on a flight, and she had break-fast in Paris, and she even raised a man from the dead.

And that was the day she learned to love the Spiral.

It all started with Dr. Pi, owner of the Sky-High Pie Shop around the corner from her home. On Wednesday—the Wednesday when everything changed—Flor was sitting in class wiggling her toes in her new pink sandals. She was staring at the clock on the wall, trying to force time to move faster. *I can't, I can't, I can't*, she was thinking. *I simply can't wait one more single second!*

Mr. Fineman, the math teacher, was in front of the shiny white board drawing large rectangles with a black marker. But Flor couldn't keep her mind on math.

It was almost three o'clock. There was no finer hour of the afternoon, especially on a Wednesday. Three o'clock on Wednesday was when the tart scent of fruit pie floated through the windows of Flor's school and did a dance right under her nose. It was the hour when Dr. Pi opened his bakery.

She could picture him. Dr. Pi lived two blocks from the water on a street paved with crooked stones, with a view of the great city of Manhattan. With a *click!* he'd turn his key in one oak door and with a *clack!* he'd turn his key in the other oak door, and then give a big shove. Now he'd call out, "Good afternoon, Brooklyn! It's three o'clock in the afternoon! Time to buy your Sky-High Pies!"

On pie day he got up at dawn. He took his morning bubble bath and slurped down his bowl of cottage cheese with ketchup. And then, while every child on the block was yawning and stretching and rubbing the sleep from their eyes, Dr. Pi padded downstairs into his shop to bake.

He filled his shop with pies once a week. They were a strange and marvelous shape. They were not flat. They were not square. They were almost not here or there. They had little pointy hills made of even littler pointy hills with berries peeking out from every point, and the whole thing going round and round and up and up to one big point at the top.

They were unbelievably yummy. You'd pinch a bit between your thumb and forefinger, just a smidge of warm crust and sweet fruit, pop it in your mouth, and let it melt on your tongue. Before you knew it you'd eaten the whole piece.

Dr. Pi was funny-looking in a friendly, comforting way. He had soft brown eyes, a big bald head, a bigger tummy, and a shy smile. He wore silk suspenders and bright button-down shirts. But the oddest thing about Dr. Pi was his hat. If you stood right in front of him it seemed like a big blue ball. If you stood behind him it looked like a small red ball. If you stood right next to him, it disappeared entirely. But when he turned around again, it popped back into view. It was such a strange hat, nobody knew what to make of it. And for that reason they politely refused to ever inquire where he'd gotten it and why it was so peculiar. They just pretended it wasn't there.

He'd been making pies for years, but no one really knew how long. He had a special recipe for piecrust, and not a soul knew what it was. He ordered his sky-high pie pans with their copper bottoms from Europe, where they were fashioned by hand by a very old man who had once been a famous sculptor. Each year he sculpted one new sky-high pie pan for Dr. Pi, and each year Dr. Pi personally delivered fresh pie to the sculptor's door.

Together they ate pie and contemplated the countryside, pie, and life. Everybody in the neighborhood adored Dr. Pi and nobody could remember a time when he hadn't lived there. But nobody could remember growing up with him either. He was simply a fact of life, like the moon and the sun.

Meanwhile, back in school, Flor's math teacher was drawing a rectangle inside a rectangle inside another rectangle. One row ahead of her, teacher's pet Nancy Know-It-All Franklin (the girl with the perfect brown hair perfectly pinned with two perfect barrettes and perfect bangs) was busy drawing exactly the same rectangles in her notebook. *Great,* thought Flor, *you get a gold medal in geek. Now make it three o'clock!*

Finally the bell rang and school was out. She jammed her books into her backpack and flew down the hall, out the door, and up the street, thinking as she did that everybody was definitely looking at her new pink sandals, which contrasted marvelously with her purple argyle knee-high socks, which were way too big and held up with green ribbons. It all clashed perfectly. *That girl has fantastic sandals,* Flor imagined the taxi driver on the corner saying. Her best friend Helen would see Flor's new sandals, say that only a fashion dunce would wear anything so *pink,* along with knee-highs so obviously donated from somebody's grandmother, and then ask if she could borrow them both.

As she turned a corner, a long, skinny shadow fell over Flor. She looked up into a frowning face. It was Mrs. Edna Plump. Mrs. Plump had once been fat, but after she went on a diet and got thin, someone nicknamed her Mrs. Plump. And for some reason humorless Mrs. Plump, who never liked a joke, loved this one and proudly began to call herself Mrs. Plump. That very same day she decided to wear only black. "Mrs. Plump always wears black," she would say. "Black is the new black. Black never goes out of fashion."

Mrs. Plump lived right next door to Dr. Pi and ran a shop called Mrs. Plump's Tea and Toast. No sugar in your tea, and no butter on your toast.

"Florence Bernoulli!" cried Mrs. Plump now. "I've heard of pink shirts and pink scarves and even fuzzy pink slippers, but pink *sandals*? On a school day? How could your mother let you out of the house?"

Suddenly it seemed very cold under Mrs. Plump's skinny shadow. For some reason Flor had never understood, Mrs. Plump seemed to take a special interest in her. Naturally, she worried that Edna Plump felt sorry for her because she lived alone with her mom. And Flor couldn't stand the thought of anybody feeling sorry for her.

"It's true," Flor said. "Only a total fashion dunce would wear pink sandals."

"Well then, Mrs. Plump has to wonder. If you know pink is inappropriate, then why are *you* wearing pink?"

"Because . . ." She thought a minute. "Because they didn't have black, Mrs. Plump. There's a long waiting list for black because *you've* made black so popular."

Mrs. Plump fell for it. "Really? Everybody is waiting for black?" She couldn't help smiling at the thought.

Of course, Mrs. Plump did not know that Flor had yellow shoes with fake fish eyes glued on top; a pair of way-too-chunky sunglasses to which she had affixed feathers from her neighbor's parrot; a rainbow of huge crinkly bowties she'd cut and sewn from old silk curtains, which she often clipped into her hair; and many other accessories too numerous to count, all of which made boring life in Brooklyn much more interesting. Flor could put on her sunglasses and hair-bowties and get into ten conversations with ten strangers on the way to the store. Mrs. Plump had no idea what fun she was missing in her world of black.

Suddenly Mrs. Plump frowned. Flor knew what was coming.

"You're not on your way to that dreadful pie shop, are you? Those pies are made of nothing but sugar and butter. Why don't you come with me instead, and let me give you a nice, healthful cup of tea and a slice of toast?"

Just then they reached the long line of pie buyers waiting outside the Sky-High Pie Shop, and Flor took her place. "I thought so," muttered Mrs. Plump, and she sneezed loudly. She held her nose with two fingers and shut her eyes. Then she marched down the street in her black high heels.

Flor could see Dr. Pi at his counter talking to a customer. Warm sunlight shone on his bald head, and a smile even warmer than the sun lit his face.

She'd known Dr. Pi since she was only a day old. Her mom loved to tell the story: "As soon as I brought you into Dr. Pi's shop to show you off, you started waving your hands in the air like a cheerleader whose team had just won. I could've sworn you two recognized each other."

But until she turned eight, her mother didn't put her in charge of buying pies. Now, at ten years old, she was the official Pie Girl.

Dr. Pi greeted Flor half an hour later, when her turn came. "We all wait for something, don't we," he said cheerfully. "Although some of us simply can't wait."

"I'm very patient," Flor said, standing on her tiptoes to get as close to the pies as possible.

"Now, Flor," scolded Dr. Pi, "you were thinking about my pies so hard that you missed your teacher's lesson on rectangles."

Flor's mouth dropped open. How did he know? "It's not my fault," she protested. "The blueberries came dancing

9

out of your pie shop and went around the block and into my classroom and ended up in front of my nose!"

He laughed. "Were they really dancing?"

Flor nodded, the tip of her chin almost touching a piecrust. "Yes, right in front of me, bouncing up and down." She inhaled the aroma of the pie. "I like this one."

"Then it's yours. This pie likes you, too."

He smiled at her. He had the warmest smile, and it always made her feel like she was wrapped in a comfy blanket. If she didn't have a real dad somewhere in France she would adopt Dr. Pi instead. She hadn't seen her real dad since she was three years old, and couldn't remember a thing about him, and so was forced to make up all kinds of stories about what he might be like so that she could almost imagine she had a fantastic French father waiting at home right this minute. For now, Dr. Pi and his shop would have to do.

Flor flopped down on a chair, kicking out her legs. Even the bottoms of her sandals were pink. She'd painted them herself, though unfortunately the paint was already flaking off. She looked outside at the line of customers, which seemed to be growing by the minute, and gulped. "Your fans have been waiting forever."

"Don't worry," he said, and pulled a pie out of the oven. "Everybody will get their pies in time. Personally, I make it a habit never to be impatient. I enjoy myself just where I am. I simply look forward to *now*. You might try that sometime."

Flor wasn't sure how you could look forward to *now*, since now was always becoming then and was totally over by the time you even noticed it. But she didn't want to point this out to Dr. Pi, as it would have been impolite.

Dr. Pi motioned to the cherry pie he'd set on the counter. "Will you help me give samples to my adoring public?" Together he and Flor cut slices of pie and brought them on a tray to the waiting customers. "By the way," he said as they came back into the shop, "your sandals are spectacular."

And then something very peculiar happened. Dr. Pi's hat began to spin. As it spun it lifted itself off his head. And he jumped like someone had just poked him hard. The color drained from his face.

"They've found me!" he exclaimed, grabbing his hat from the air with both hands and running into the back of his shop. The door slammed behind him.

Should she go after him? Who had found him? And why was he running away? Well, this was certainly very exciting.

"Hello, miss? Are you listening or daydreaming? I'm in a hurry and I'd like that one," a man said as he wheeled his bicycle into the shop and pointed to a blackberry pie.

"Well, I—I—"

"I'm a very important person in a terrible *rush*. Can't you *see* that?"

"Yes, sir, you look more rushed than any man I've ever seen, but how important you really are I have no idea—"

"Miss! Just do your job and get me *that* pie there. *That's* the one I want."

She sighed. "You've picked the best pie of them all, so . . . please just be a little *patient* while I get it out."

Flor slid the pie onto a sheet of wax paper, sprinkled brown sugar over the top, and packed it up in a box, the way she'd seen Dr. Pi do every Wednesday of every week of her life. Not a moment later, the next customer stepped up and Flor took his order.

About twenty minutes later Dr. Pi reappeared. The color had returned to his face and his hat was back to normal, but he looked worried. "You've saved me! I can't thank you enough. By the way," he said, as he beckoned to another customer, "your mother is having guests to dinner tonight."

"We're not having guests," Flor assured him. "She doesn't like to cook. She's the Chinese menu takeout queen." Then she put on her best imitation "Mom" accent. "Triple Jade Delight? General Tso's Chicken?"

"I'm certain you two are having guests," he repeated. "I think she'd be pleased if you brought home two pies."

Flor shook her head, mystified. "How do you do that?"

"Do what?"

"Know what's going to happen before it happens? Or know what happened when you weren't even there—like my math teacher talking about rectangles. How do you do it?"

"It's not hard," he said as he handed a customer a pie. "I just take a peek around the curve."

"A peek around *what* curve?"

"The curve of time," he said, as if the idea that time was curved was the most natural thing, like bubbles in soda.

"Dr. Pi, that's a joke. Time just marches ahead, day after day, year after year," Flor said with great confidence, as she packed a pie into a box. "It goes right from the past straight into the future."

"It doesn't curve?" he inquired.

"Nope."

"And it never goes backward?"

"Of course not, or you could change the past. And you never can change the past. Like my mom says, 'You can regret the past, but you can't change it!'"

He packed two more pies. "Well, you're sort of right and yet not quite. Time does, in fact, move forward. But it does not go in a straight line. Time curves. So I can take a peek around the curve, sort of like looking around the corner. So that's how I know you're having strangers to dinner tonight."

"Well, where is this curve? Can I take a look?"

"Soon!" he said brightly. "You'll be peeking around that curve yourself in no time."

And that was that. Flor really wanted to see that curve, or look around it, as it sounded amazingly useful, the kind of thing that could completely change your life forever, but before she could even blink they had served the last customer and Dr. Pi said, "I've got so much more to tell you and we've only got about five minutes before your mother is going to start worrying about you."

"What about the police?" she whispered.

"The police?"

"Are you running from the law? Who's after you?"

He looked surprised, then threw his head back and laughed so hard his stomach shook. "Oh no, Flor. No, no, no. Not the police. Although," he sighed, "I wish it were that simple."

Dr. Pi took her hands and looked at her very gravely. "It's my recipe, you see."

"You're afraid somebody will steal your recipe?"

"My recipe is based on a math equation. And, I might add, a lovely equation at that." He paused and looked away dreamily. "It has hypnotized many a man before me."

"Ummm . . . I'm sorry, but I have *no* idea what you're talking about."

"I didn't invent the equation."

Flor just decided to roll with it, since Dr. Pi was making no sense. After all, he *was* on the run from somebody, and maybe he'd temporarily lost his mind. So she said gently, as if trying to soothe a child who'd just awakened from a bad dream, "What does this have to do with the recipe?"

Dr. Pi shook his head. "I thought a pie shop was the perfect hiding place. I thought I was so clever. I'm afraid that I was wrong."

Chapter 2

A PEEK AROUND THE CURVE OF TIME

I've got to slow time just a little more, or I won't have any time," Dr. Pi said as he turned an oak wheel behind his counter that Flor had never noticed before. It looked like a steering wheel on a pirate ship. She could almost feel time slowing down. The air grew gooey and sticky. She felt sleepy.

"Hey, this is pretty cool," she said. "I could use this trick when I'm doing homework, since I never have enough time. How'd you do it?"

He smiled. "That's a special time-slowing wheel I got for my birthday long ago. I've used it many a morning when I had too many pies to bake and too little time in which to bake them. Here's another one you'll like." He began to unfold his hat. "I've wanted to show someone this trick for years. It's been lonely keeping so many secrets to myself!"

The hat got bigger and rounder and bigger and rounder until it was so enormous he put it on the floor upside down. Flor climbed up on a chair, and then onto the counter, stretched up high, and looked over the edge. She could hardly see the bottom.

"If you jumped, you could fall for days!" she joked.

"Look closer," he instructed her, "and you'll see a pocket inside the hat. Unzip it."

She did, and out came a little staircase that began to unfold, or rather, unroll.

"Awesome!"

"Give it a tap and it'll roll right back up."

She did, and zipped the pocket shut. Next to the zipper was a label.

"'Crafted from the Finest Felt,'" Flor read out loud, squinting. "'Made of Rectangles, Planes, and Curves, with

Extra Special Strings and Speeds.'" She looked up. "Is this for real or am I dreaming? Who gave you this hat—the same person who gave you that wheel for slowing time?"

He laughed. "They have both been passed down from generation to generation in my family for so long we don't even know where they first came from. Now watch *this* trick," he said, and gave a shove and a push and a tug and began to fold the hat up. It grew smaller and smaller until it was the size of a berry. And there it sat in his hand, his teeny tiny round hat.

"Wow," she said, her mouth a wide-open O of wonder, "that silly hat is so small now that a housefly could wear it out to dinner."

"This hat has saved my life a few times. Now," he went on, lowering his voice, "I have a favor to ask. How about if you keep it for a while?"

She frowned. "You're never without that hat."

"Did you see how it flew off my head?"

"Yeah," she admitted.

"I would like you to keep it for me. Clearly it wants to be off of me."

He held out his hand. She took the little bead of a hat and dropped it into her pocket.

"You are full of surprises today," she commented.

"I was going to explain everything to you next year," he said. "I thought I'd invite you and your mom over for pie and . . . well, anyway . . ." He motioned Flor to follow him down a long hallway to a room looking out on his garden, where birds were splashing in a bowl of water under a gingko tree. On a single table sat a giant seashell.

"You see, Flor, I am in charge of the Spiral," Dr. Pi said very solemnly.

"Oh?" she said, staring at the gleaming shell.

"The logarithmic Spiral."

"The logga what?"

"The logarithmic Spiral. Or you can call it the miraculous Spiral, as your own ancestor—I mean, as somebody very smart—once said."

Flor just stared at Dr. Pi. Her darling Dr. Pi, who'd apparently lost his mind.

He went on, "A spiral is different from a square or a circle or a rectangle."

"Obviously, but who doesn't know that?"

He continued, "This Spiral is one-of-a-kind. It gets bigger and bigger without changing its shape at all. Do you know anything else that can do that?"

"No," she admitted.

"Here, let me show you."

And he sat down to draw a spiral for her.

"I've seen a spiral before. And, well, that's very nice and all, but to tell the truth, Dr. Pi, I like pies and clothes and my cat Libenits. I guess I'll leave the spiral business to you."

"This Spiral is already part of your life, Flor," said Dr. Pi.

Flor stared. Now he really wasn't making any sense.

"It is a very important spiral. And I am in charge of it!" he said, looking worried. "I keep the math formula for the Spiral inside this table." Suddenly he got down on his knees and crawled underneath the table. He opened a compartment and took out a piece of paper filled with equations and symbols and stood up and handed it to Flor. "This is the formula I use to bake my Sky-High

21

Pies. Haven't you ever noticed their spiral shape?"

"Dr. Pi, I already sat through one math class today," Flor said. "I pretty much hate math. I'm sure Mr. Fineman will start teaching us about spirals soon enough."

"Flor, you don't hate math," he said gently.

"Don't you think it's more important to find out who's after you right now?"

He frowned. "You'll meet them tonight."

"I will?" She tapped her foot a little impatiently. "Maybe I should go home and change into something fancy for the event! When are they coming back?" *And,* she wanted to add, *when are you going to come back to your senses?*

But he seemed oblivious to his own madness. "Soon enough . . . well, to make a long story short, I make sure the Spiral keeps spiraling. I make sure it has enough fire. I can't let the fire go out, you see. It's my job."

Maybe, thought Flor, if she asked him very specific questions, ones he couldn't answer, he'd realize he had temporarily gone insane. He'd shake his head, blink his eyes, look embarrassed, and be himself again.

"So, Dr. Pi," she asked, in her best police officer imitation, "who gave you this job?"

"That's a long tale."

"Well then, Dr. Pi," she continued sternly, "what happens if the fire goes out?"

"Then the Spiral stops spiraling."

"Aha! The Spiral stops spiraling. I see! And then what happens?"

"And then everything that is made of spirals, like seashells and snails and galaxies, wouldn't know how to grow or turn properly."

She was getting nowhere. Flor made one last desperate attempt at reason: "I suppose the fire for this Spiral is sitting somewhere, like, in some fire-only supermarket on Mars, right?"

Dr. Pi shook his head. "Oh dear, Flor, I see you don't believe me at all. I think you can only understand if you experience it."

"Well, I'm not sure I want to," she said crossly. "Anyway, Dr. Pi, please tell me who is after you and why. Maybe I can help."

"Well, naturally, when you protect something valuable, there are going to be people who want to steal it."

Just then the doorbell rang. Flor practically jumped into the air. It was almost like some little part of her believed every crazy word he'd said. "Who could it be?" she breathed.

He looked puzzled. "Honestly, I don't think . . . but . . . let me go see." He hesitated. "You wait here."

Her face fell. "And miss the excitement?"

"I promise if anything interesting starts to happen, you'll be the first to know."

With nothing much to do except wait, Flor walked over to the gleaming shell on the table. It had a pearly glow and pinkish stripes across its curving surface.

"I guess it's no coincidence," she said to herself, "that it's shaped like a spiral." She knew from science class that this was a nautilus shell. The creature who lived inside started out small, but as it outgrew its chamber, it would build a new chamber and seal off the old one. It would do this time and time again, as it got bigger and bigger. And the chambers joined together in the form of a spiral—round and round.

Flor had never seen a shell this big, though. It took up the entire table. She peered into the gleaming interior. She could almost hear the wind and sea. And suddenly she saw something. An image on the interior of the shell, like someone somewhere had a tiny movie camera. A lady in black. She looked closer. A very familiar lady in black climbing over a brick wall.

"Dr. Pi, it's Mrs. Plump!" she shouted. "And she's climbing over your back wall! I think she's spying on you."

But Dr. Pi was still in the front of the shop. He didn't hear her.

Suddenly Flor wasn't questioning spirals or seashells or Dr. Pi's sanity or the very strange turn of events her life had suddenly taken this afternoon. After all, when magic strikes, at some point you just go straight for the magic. Life hadn't been *this* fabulous in a long, long time. Flor stuck her head in farther. Now the invisible movie projector showed her two skinny blond men eating dinner in her own home! Their chins were long and sharp. They looked identical except she could see through one of them, right to the other side.

Could these be the unexpected guests Dr. Pi was talking about?

She felt a tap on her shoulder.

"Yes," she heard Dr. Pi saying, "those are your mother's unexpected guests."

She turned around. "Who are they?"

"The brothers, Mr. Bit and Mr. It. I believe they've come to steal the fire for the Spiral."

"Steal it?" She looked back at the shell. "Does that thing tell the future? Is that what you meant by looking around the curve of time?"

He nodded. "It's a little more complicated than that, but in a word, yes. By the way, Flor, do you know a girl named Lucy? About your age? Short blond hair, and yea big—or small, actually. She's a pixie."

"Nope," said Flor, still staring at the magic shell. She didn't look up as she answered. "Never heard of her."

"She says she's going to be your best friend soon. She said she promised to prove it to you, and this is proof. She wanted a pie for her dad, who according to her is 'madder than a wet hen and laid up in bed after his tractor adopted a tree.' I think it means he crashed into a tree while on his tractor and he's in a really bad mood. But who in Brooklyn rides a tractor?"

"You got me," Flor said, and shrugged. "Dr. Pi, about the shell—"

"In just a minute," he said. "You see, I gave Lucy a pie and told her that I hope her dad enjoys it. But she insisted on meeting you, so I let her come on in for a minute."

"So where is she?" said Flor.

"Right behind you, silly!" came a light, cheerful voice with a distinct southern drawl.

Flor looked up. The voice came from a girl about her age but much smaller, with short blond hair that she had apparently styled herself into spikes. *She probably thinks those spikes are cool*, thought Flor, *but they're totally uncool.*

"Who are you?"

"Lucy Eastwood," the girl said amiably, pulling a candy bar out of her back pocket. She was wearing jeans, a white shirt, a vest, and cowboy boots. She stuck out her hand, offering the candy bar to Flor.

"No thanks," said Flor.

"Why not?"

"Why would I eat a candy bar when I can eat home-made pie?" Flor said, in a purposely pitying tone.

Lucy didn't seem fazed. "You don't have to eat it. You just have to take it and keep it."

"No, I don't have to do anything." She didn't know why this girl annoyed her so much. Maybe it was the ridiculous cowboy outfit.

"But you really do," Lucy said, and started laughing. She had an amazingly deep laugh for such a pipsqueak of a girl. It boomed out like a clap of joyous thunder.

"Why's that?" Flor was so irritated she almost forgot about the magic shell.

"You keep it until we meet again and I ask you for it. In fact, whatever you do, don't eat it! And I've got to be running back to the future now, so please, just take my candy bar."

Flor looked at Dr. Pi, who seemed quite unsurprised by this incredibly strange girl.

"You might as well take it," Dr. Pi said.

"Where are you from?" Flor said suspiciously. "Not from Brooklyn, that's for sure."

"'Course not," said Lucy. "Not in a million years would I ever be from Brooklyn."

"So?"

"I'm from Adel," said Lucy.

"Where's that?"

"Adel, Georgia. I raise my own chickens and pick my own figs off trees in my backyard. My dad owns the ice factory. We make snow in the summer if you want! We make one hundred and fifty thousand pounds of ice a day. My dad will love this pie. He's never had a pie shaped like this. Bye-bye for now!"

She handed Flor the candy bar. Flor was too astonished to say more. She just stood there, wordless, while Lucy practically ran out the door.

"What was that all about, Dr. Pi?" she demanded.

"I guess you'll find out later," he said. "That's what she said, anyway. But for now, it's time to take your pies home to your mother. Tomorrow you can stop by before school and tell me everything you've learned about Mr. Bit and

Mr. It. It's very important. Oh," he added, "and don't forget to do *all* your homework."

"I won't," she promised. "But there's one thing I don't understand."

"What's that, Flor?"

"Even if you're not crazy or a criminal or something, why did you tell *me* all this? Why would Mr. It and Mr. Bit come to *my* house? I'm just an ordinary ten-year-old girl."

"We are related, Flor," he said. "And our destinies are linked." He looked deep into her eyes. "One day, and not such a far-off day, you will know who you are."

She looked at him in disbelief.

"I'm . . . uh . . . Florence Bernoulli. . . . I live on Joralemon Street . . . in Brooklyn Heights. . . . I'm ten years old. . . ." Her voice trailed off.

"You're a *Bernoulli*," he emphasized. And that was all he would say, as he wrapped up her pies and ushered her out into the street.

Chapter
3

MRS. PLUMP MAKES A PLAN

It has to stop, and I'm clearly the one who has to stop it," Mrs. Edna Plump muttered to herself after she left Flor outside Dr. Pi's shop. She stepped into her own Tea and Toast shop next door, and wondered why the world did not appreciate her own style and wisdom just a bit more. Instead they were practically drunk with the delight of pies. They had no discipline. They did not appreciate virtue, modesty, and simplicity. They did not understand that tea and toast were far more than snacks, they represented a whole way of life. People were simply gluttons!

She loved her little shop. Behind the counter were stacks of gold and silver tea tins from all over the world, and just as many tins of packaged toast—rye toast, white toast, corn toast, rice toast. Along the wall were twenty wooden chairs at twenty tiny tables where several ladies sat, dressed in black. They were her loyal customers. They were her flock. They came to learn how to diet and lose weight, but they learned much, much more. They learned a whole philosophy of life. The Way of Tea and Toast. Mrs. Plump waved to them and poured herself a cup of jasmine tea. "Ah," she said, breathing the fragrant steam. With two fingers she pinched off a piece of dry toast and began to munch. Munch. Munch. Munch. A few flakes fell onto her saucer, and she pressed a wet fingertip to each one and licked it off.

"Chew twenty times," she said to the ladies, who nodded and began to chomp on their morsels of toast. "You begin to digest your food as soon as you start to chew it. So chew twenty times before you swallow. Now remember, you came here to lose weight. And what is your motto?"

"We lose the most with tea and toast!" the ladies sang. "With tea and toast, we lose the most!"

Mrs. Plump smiled. "We are tea-and-toasters! And what is our other motto?"

"Black is the new black!"

"Perfection, ladies. We wear black because it makes us look so slim." She sipped her tea and sighed. "Ladies, I am troubled. I need your thoughtful wisdom."

The ladies leaned forward.

"Just now I saw that neighborhood girl, Flor, leave Dr. Pi's Sky-High Pie Shop with *two* pies."

"Oh no!" gasped the ladies.

"Oh yes! And each pie was over two feet tall."

"Not so!"

"Just so! Next week it will be three pies, the week after it will be four. Soon she'll forget all about real food and eat nothing but pies for breakfast, lunch, and dinner."

The ladies set down their teacups, outraged. One of them said, "It must be her French blood. Her mother was married to a French painter. And you know what wonderful chefs the French are."

"Poor girl," said another. "Her parents divorced when she was just a baby and her father went back to France. Now Flor lives alone with her mother and a cat. They probably console themselves with pies."

"It isn't all *that* bad," said a third lady. "I hear her mother is a fashion photographer. She goes to wonderful parties all around town."

Mrs. Plump broke in. "So? What is your point?"

The ladies didn't have a point.

"Ladies," Mrs. Plump said, "there was a time when I was quite plump." She paused dramatically. Her voice dropped to a whisper. "It is the inner self, the soul that matters. We should never judge another by appearance." Then she shook her head and went on primly, "But ladies, does that mean we let this sweet girl go the way of all plumpness? Eating pies full of butter and sugar? When she could have a healthy snack of tea and toast? I can't let it happen to another girl like I once was. I will close up early today. As you can see, this is an emergency I must attend to."

And with that, she said good-bye to each lady, gently

pushed them, one by one, out the door, and put up a sign, CLOSED UNTIL TOMORROW.

Alone, she sat down and opened a large notebook. It was filled with neat entries over many months in her own handwriting.

"Wednesday," read the first entry. "Apricot is the flavor this week. Dr. Pi sold forty apricot pies today. Two of my ladies fell off their diets on the way past his shop. They could not help buying a pie."

"Wednesday," read another entry. "Raspberry. Dr. Pi sold ninety raspberry pies today. Three of my ladies fell off their diets on the way past his shop. I have too many bills to pay. I must raise the price of my tea."

"Wednesday. Dr. Pi sold one hundred banana pies today. Four more of my ladies fell off their diets on the way past his shop. I must raise the price of my toast."

"Thursday. I had no choice. I climbed over Dr. Pi's wall into his backyard last night. It was not easy in my black dress and heels. I looked in every window, but I did not see any pie tins. I did see Dr. Pi in his pajamas, reading a book."

"Friday. Why did I do it? Perhaps I was just bored to tears. I had already straightened all my tea tins. I had already washed every last teacup. There wasn't a speck of dirt. There wasn't a crumb anywhere. But it was hours until bedtime and nothing to do. So I climbed over Dr. Pi's wall again last night. I broke the heel of my shoe. I slept in the garden with the worms. Dr. Pi came downstairs at five in the morning. I saw him reading his recipe. It must be a very long recipe, as it's on an extremely large piece of paper."

Now Mrs. Edna Plump made a new entry. "Wednesday again. Dr. Pi sold all his blueberry pies today. I saw Flor with *two* pies. What is our neighborhood coming to? I will break in tonight while he is sleeping and steal his recipe. I am sure he doesn't know it by heart because it's so long. Without his recipe, what can he do?" She paused, her pen in midair, a smile on her long, lonely face. Then she added one more line: "Perhaps I can use his recipe to make toast that goes round and round and up and up like those sky-high pies that all of Brooklyn seems to love so much. Toast that turns! That's what I'll call it! It will be a smashing success and help me pay my bills."

She closed the book and stood. "When the going gets tough, the tough drink tea!" she said to nobody in particular. It would have been nice if someone was around to listen, especially at night. But she had been alone for many more years than she could count, and she was quite used to talking with herself, and giving herself good advice.

Tough times like these called for Red Hot Tea of Night, seasoned with chili peppers. She brewed a big pot. She drank it down like water. Fire burned in her blood. It was time to put the good Dr. Pi out of business. It was time to save Flor Bernoulli from death by pies.

Mrs. Plump was on a mission.

Chapter

4

TWO GUESTS MAKE A CRASH LANDING

As Flor stepped onto the landing of the top floor of the brownstone where she lived, she found herself gazing up at the stained-glass skylight. Sun poured through the glass like a blessing, tossing petals of color everywhere. Her dad, Jacques, had crafted it after he married her mom. He must have been feeling very romantic at the time, because he chose purples, blues, and rich, deep reds. Flor liked to hop on one foot on a single color—from purple to purple, from blue to blue, until she reached the half flight of stairs that led to her apartment door. Sometimes, when nobody was looking, she pressed the palm of her hand to her lips and placed that hand on a frond of color, a kind of "kiss" for him.

She put down her bag of pies and stood there, catching her breath. Visions of Dr. Pi's whirling hat, of the magic shell and the curve of time and Mrs. Plump scrambling over the wall, and the two skinny blond strangers tumbled behind her eyes. In fact, her insides felt very much like socks in a hot clothes dryer.

She went inside, through a living room with colorful Mexican rugs, past the piano with its trill of white keys, down a long hallway, and into the glass-enclosed terrace of their rooftop apartment. There, floor-to-ceiling windows offered a view of Manhattan. On a bright day like today, the city across the river looked exactly like rock crystal.

Her mom was standing at the windows, eating an apple. She was wearing a long white shirt and black spangled leggings and her thick, wavy red hair was tied into a ponytail. Libenits was asleep on his silk pillow. As soon as Flor came in he opened his yellow eyes, yawned, and ambled over for a scratch behind the ears.

"Hello, darling," her mother said. "I was pretending I was in Paris. If you kind of squint, so you don't see much at all, you can almost fool yourself into thinking that's the River Seine, not the East River."

Flor sighed. She was pretty well convinced her mom had never gotten over her dad. Why else would she be pretending she was in Paris?

"I'm sorry I'm so late," Flor began, but stopped at her mother's puzzled look. "Am I late, Mom?" she asked.

"No, you're right on time. How is Dr. Pi?"

Flor wasn't sure how to answer that question. Should she say, "Dr. Pi might have lost his mind and asked me to make sure the fire in the Spiral never goes out?" Nope, she wouldn't understand (Flor barely did). Better just to say, "The same as ever, Mom. I brought home two pies today."

"Oh, you're bad," her mother said with a smile.

"In case we have guests," Flor explained.

Just then there was a loud crash and the sound of breaking glass.

"What was that?" exclaimed her mother.

But Flor knew.

A moment later the doorbell rang.

"Who could that be?" her mother continued, puzzled.

Oh yes, Flor really knew. This was unbelievable, knowing things ahead of time! Had she really looked around the curve of time? With her heart pounding so fast she could hardly breathe, she ran down the hallway and skidded to a stop before the front door.

She heard them arguing.

"Mr. It!"

"What, Mr. Bit?"

"Is that what you call a safe landing?"

"Of course. We're both still alive."

"We flew all night and crashed through a skylight, and this is certainly not a pie shop."

"You try to steer across two galaxies and through six wormholes and make a soft landing, too."

"Five wormholes, Mr. It. Five, and we're barely alive."

"Okay, five wormholes."

Flor opened the door to see the two tall blond twin brothers she expected. They were wearing white suits, white shirts, and white ties. Even their shoes were white. When they saw her, their eyebrows lifted high and their mouths fell open and they looked as astonished as she herself felt. They were exactly the same, except the one called Mr. Bit was transparent. She could actually see through to the wall behind him. He was there, but at the same time, he sort of wasn't. How odd.

As soon as he overcame his astonishment, the one called Mr. It apologized. "So sorry to disturb you, miss. This is your home and we were looking for a business establishment. I see we've destroyed your skylight, but we will purchase you a new one tomorrow."

"What a disaster!" her mother, who was right behind her, cried out, looking in dismay at the stairway filled with broken glass. Then she saw the two men. Quickly she put her arm around Flor and lied, "We have a burglar alarm that goes right to the police station. So the police will be here any minute."

"You see, I haven't perfected a proper landing," said Mr. It, his face pink with embarrassment. "We don't travel much."

"A proper landing?" Flor's mother repeated in disbelief.

"Did you ever think of ringing a doorbell?" Flor inquired.

"Or taking stairs?" Flor's mother echoed. "Ever hear of stairs?" She started to pull Flor back into the apartment and shut the door. "I'm calling the police."

"Wait, Mom," said Flor.

"Wait for what?"

"Just please, wait a second. Maybe they're . . . maybe they're not burglars."

"We're not burglars," Mr. Bit yelled through the door. "We are just looking for Pi."

"We have pie right here!" Flor said brightly, opening the door. "Are you hungry?"

"I'm never hungry," Mr. Bit said, as if slightly insulted.

"Actually, I'm starved," said Mr. It. "It's been a long trip and I feel faint. And besides, Mr. Bit, where a pie is, a pie maker is not far behind."

"Flor!" said her mother sharply. "Are you trying to invite these strangers, who just destroyed our skylight, to dinner?"

"We have extra pie, Mom. And they said they'd buy us a new skylight."

"Absolutely not."

"We won't stay, ma'am, of course not," said Mr. It. "But let us at least clean up our mess."

"That's a job for professionals. There are hundreds of pieces of broken glass here. You'd cut yourself," said Flor's mother.

"Mr. Bit never cuts himself, and it's the least we can do."

"I can't be cut," said Mr. Bit. "That's because I'm neither here nor there." He bent down and scooped up pieces of glass in his hands. They seemed to pierce his see-through skin, even poke through it, but he just laughed. "Doesn't hurt at all," he said. He held the jagged heaps of glass as easily as a bunch of flowers. He dumped them into a garbage pail on the landing and scooped up another handful. Then he got down on his knees and picked up every last tiny morsel of glass, all with ease and speed.

"Wow!" said Flor. She turned to her mom. "Come on, Mom!"

Her mom stared at the garbage pail in disbelief.

"So," said Mr. Bit, brushing off the sleeves of his suit jacket and grinning a big sort of goofy, proud grin. "All cleaned up."

"I must be out of my mind," said Flor's mother, but Flor could see that something about the twins had swayed her in their favor. "All right then, come in for a piece of pie."

Chapter
5

MR. BIT JUST DON'T FIT

They must have invented the phrase "fussy eater" for Mr. Bit, Flor thought. He sat at his plate moving a forkful of pie back and forth, as if he were conducting a science experiment. He stared at it, smushed it, picked off a blueberry and pushed it away, lifted the fork to his nose to sniff, took a tiny lick, then put it back down and looked around as if bored.

"Mr. Bit, you don't seem very hungry," said Flor's mom.

"I'm Mr. Bit, I'm in a snit," he pouted. In fact, he looked very peeved.

But his twin, Mr. It, practically shivered with delight. He opened his mouth as wide as he could—*as wide,* thought Flor, *as you do at the dentist's*—and then shoveled pie into it.

"I wish you didn't have to stop and eat all the time," complained Mr. Bit. "It's almost a crime. You eat every single day! And besides, it's so boring. I'd have more fun sleeping and snoring."

"If you only knew what you were missing. If only you didn't survive on air and possibility."

Mr. Bit pouted even more. "Your obsession with food is one of your worst idiot-syncracies."

"He likes wordplay, doesn't he?" murmured Flor's mom.

Mr. It nodded. "He finds it easier to think in jokes and rhymes."

"It's true, I do. I rhyme all the time," said Mr. Bit. "Well, not all the time. But I love to rhyme!" He turned to Mr. It. "Brother, give me a rhyme!"

"Not now. Another time," Mr. It begged off.

Mr. Bit grinned. "Very clever. You're a brother like no other."

"Well," said Flor, "at least you two get along. So where do you come from? And how did you happen to crash through our skylight?"

Mr. Bit looked at Mr. It. Mr. It looked at Flor. Flor looked at her mom.

"Well?" asked her mom, staring at the men.

"Yes. Umm. Well. Ma'am," Mr. It said, "the long and short of it is . . . we traveled across two galaxies and crashed through six wormholes."

"Five," said Mr. Bit.

"Five," Mr. It echoed.

"You're not serious?" said her mom. "You think we're in a science fiction movie?"

"You did crash through the skylight," said Flor. Then she frowned. "But where's your spaceship?"

"We folded it up as soon as we hit Earth's atmosphere, of course," said Mr. Bit.

"I see," said Flor, though she didn't.

"We've come in search of Pi."

"You have pie right here," said Flor's mom.

"No, my dear lady, not pie. *Pi!*" he emphasized.

48

Flor's mom shook her head. And then suddenly it dawned on her. "You mean Dr. Pi?"

"Yes, of course!" Mr. Bit chimed in. "But why do you call him a doctor? Is he one?"

"Why are you looking for him, anyway?" Flor asked.

Mr. Bit turned to his twin. "I'm at a loss. You're the boss." And with that he slid back into his chair, shrugged, and waved at Mr. It.

"I'd be pleased to tell you whatever you'd like to know," said Mr. It politely.

"For starters, where are you from?"

"A faraway galaxy not unlike your own."

"Well, how did you get here?"

"We used the typical shortcuts. We folded space and stepped across it, and took every convenient wormhole we could find."

"I see," said Flor again, though once again she didn't. "How long have you been chasing Dr. Pi?"

"Chasing?" echoed Mr. It. "I wouldn't put it exactly like that."

"Just answer the question, please," said Flor politely.

"If it's a chase, it's our first chase," Mr. It said.

"And our last, I'm sure," said Mr. Bit.

"We've come to make a visit and ask a favor," said Mr. It.

"But what do you want from Dr. Pi?" asked Flor's mom.

"He has fire. We need a little."

"You want to steal the fire," Flor said triumphantly. "Don't you?"

"We don't want to steal anything. We were going to ask ever so politely."

"And surely Pi can spare it," added Mr. Bit. "Why, he uses it for mere meaningless pies!"

"He can't spare it," said Flor. "And if he refuses when you ask him so politely, you're just going to steal it. Aren't you? You didn't fly through six wormholes—"

"Five," interrupted Mr. Bit.

"Okay, five wormholes, you didn't fly through five whole wormholes just to ask a favor, and if it's refused, go home!"

"My brother needs it!" Mr. Bit said, springing to his feet. "Where is Pi?" he cried in his tin-metal voice.

"Dr. Pi will never stop guarding the Spiral!" Flor burst out.

"The Spiral!" said her mother. "Did you say *the Spiral*?"

"The Spiral," echoed Mr. Bit. "I'm a fan of a good old-fashioned spiral, but what does that have to do with the fire?"

"Why, the Spiral needs fire, of course," said Flor.

Mr. Bit peered at her.

"You're saying he's the Keeper of the Spiral?" he asked suspiciously.

Flor nodded. "Exactly."

Mr. Bit turned to his brother. "This is not good. Not good at all. He's not going to want to give us even one lick of fire."

Mr. It nodded. "But we have to try. Can you check the latitude and longitude again? We'd better visit him now." He turned to Flor's mom and bowed. It seemed really old-fashioned and yet somehow gallant. "Thank you for the delicious pie."

"I didn't mean to get upset," Mr. Bit apologized to Flor. He walked to the front door and looked up at the hole where the skylight had been. It was evening, and a full moon was pinned to the sky. "Why do I lose my cool? I'm perfect up there," said Bit. "But down here, where you all live, I don't fit. Bit don't fit. I make a mess. I lose my way. I say some things I shouldn't say."

Chapter 6

FLOR DRESSES FOR THE NIGHT OF NIGHTS

Flor didn't know what to think. Her mom didn't say another word about Mr. Bit and Mr. It. Not a word about the Spiral. Nothing—nada—about fixing the smashed skylight. She just shook her head and carried the pie plates into the kitchen, as if two ordinary neighbors had visited and maybe stayed a little too long. In fact, she seemed to be in a daze.

"Time for me to catch up on some phone calls and for you to do your homework, Miss Flor," she said, brushing her daughter's curls back from her face. Like her mother, Flor had green eyes and unruly red hair. "Then we'll order Chinese takeout since we missed dinnertime. I'm going to have Moo Shu Vegetable and Spicy Shrimp Soup."

"I'll have Creaky Chicken," said Flor, "with extra hot pepper sauce."

"Okay." Her mother held out Flor's backpack. "See you in an hour?"

"Sure," said Flor. "But, Mom, uh . . ."

Her mother waited patiently. Flor really wanted to ask her mother why she'd been shocked—and yet not entirely surprised—about the Spiral. What did her mom know that she wasn't talking about?

"Well . . . ummm . . . nothing, I guess."

"See you in an hour, then?"

"All right."

Flor went into her room and dumped her schoolbooks on the bed. She reached into her pocket and took out the candy bar that strange pipsqueak of a girl from Adel, Georgia, had given her. She was about to throw it out, but then decided to put it on her desk instead. She took out her math homework.

It was hard to concentrate on math at the best of times, but tonight it was impossible.

"I'm stuck doing homework and waiting for the same old Chinese food I eat every night, while the most fantastic adventure that has ever happened in my whole life is happening without me!" she grumbled to herself.

Her mom had always said, *Take a chance. It's the roads you didn't walk down that you wonder about. It's the doors you didn't open that you regret.* Well, on this ordinary Wednesday a once-in-a-lifetime door had opened, and she simply couldn't let it shut forever while she did homework.

The question, of course, was what to wear before she snuck out. Flor slid the closet door open. How about those black palazzo pants, with their flared legs and foldover waist? Platform shoes and one clip-on earring? Thrift shop lace draped across the shoulder, on the bias, as they say? A Batman cape?

She examined this new outfit in the mirror. This was one her friends were going to borrow like mad. It was half-Halloween and half high-style. Quickly she got out her notebook, wrote down what she was wearing, and labeled her new outfit, "Spiral-Saving Ensemble." Then she snapped a picture and uploaded it to her laptop.

As she was putting away her school clothes, Dr. Pi's all-but-forgotten, teeny-tiny hat fell out of her pocket and rolled across her floor. With each roll it got bigger. She snatched it up just in time to put it on her head. And somehow it made the outfit. An outfit like this might be a finalist for France. She had a secret plan to fly to Paris and find her father on her sixteenth birthday. So far she had five outfits planned for her trip.

Flor took a marker and wrote a note, "I went over to Dr. Pi's, be back soon," and taped it to her door. She'd never snuck out on her mother, but quietly now, ever so quietly, she slipped into the front hallway. The door to her mom's bedroom was ajar, and she was on the phone.

"That's exactly what I want to know," her mother was saying. "Out of nowhere she brings up a spiral. And Jacques signed his artwork with a spiral instead of his name. He never forgot to include it. He said he was honoring his ancestors. He's a descendant of one of the most famous math families in history."

Her mother was silent, as if listening. Then she answered. "The Bernoullis. It sounds like a Mafia family, doesn't it? They lived in Basel during the seventeenth and eighteenth centuries. Well, they are still alive, apparently. And some of them are still mathematicians. Flor spooked me, she really did, when she said Dr. Pi would never stop guarding the Spiral. What made her say that?"

This was eavesdropping heaven, and Flor wanted nothing more than to stay, pressed against the wall outside her mother's room. Especially since the conversation included her dad. But she could feel—in her bones, head, tongue, and feet, like the far-off rumble of a train or storm—she could just *feel* things happening at this very moment without her.

So she walked down the hall and out the front door, shutting it as softly as possible. The pail of broken glass was still there, the last and only evidence that her father had ever lived here.

Flor loved her quiet street, with its elegant brick row houses, flower boxes, and stone stoops the color of toffee. At the very end, toward the harbor, were blue-gray stones from a time long before anybody had invented cars, when New York was filled with horse-drawn carriages. *Clickety-clack, clickety-clack.* She could almost hear it.

Dr. Pi's shop was locked, and the windows were dark. Next door, a big sign hung on the door of Mrs. Plump's Tea and Toast: CLOSED UNTIL TOMORROW. Flor stood in front of the two shops. Either the brothers Bit and It had already come and kidnapped Dr. Pi, or they were completely lost. What the heck was she going to do?

"Nice hat," said a woman walking by.

"You like it?"

"I more than like it. I love it. Who made it?"

"It's one-of-a-kind," said Flor proudly, removing the hat to show it off.

Just then a copper key fell out of the hat and clattered on the ground. It had two teeth at the end, as well as a lot of filigree and curves.

Flor picked it up and said hastily, "I've been looking all over for that key!"

The woman smiled and went off down the street.

When a key falls out of a magic hat, it obviously wants

to open something. The key was warm in her hand. She turned it over. Engraved on the back were strange words.

"*Eadem mutata resurgo semperdem,*" she said slowly. "What does that mean?"

Well, there was no treasure chest anywhere in sight, so she marched up to Dr. Pi's double oak doors. The key slipped right in. Flor entered the dark, deserted pie shop, and shut the doors behind her.

Chapter
7

MR. BIT SMASHES A SEASHELL

The shop was as silent as a cemetery at two in the morning. You could almost hear a speck of dust drift to the floor. Taking Dr. Pi's hat off, Flor unzipped the flap, dropped the key in, zipped it up, and put the hat back on. She then pulled off her platform shoes, placed them side by side near the door, and padded as quietly as a cat into the back room. The fortune-telling seashell gleamed on the table, as if shining in its own light.

She switched on the light and ran both hands down the shell's pearly curves. Just as she was about to stick her head inside, there was a thud in the garden. Not a moment later a very messy Mrs. Plump—her dress covered with dirt and grass, and her sleeve torn—struggled to her feet and stood on the other side of the window, looking at Flor. Her mouth was a round O of astonishment.

"Flor Bernoulli, what are you doing here at night?"

"What are *you* doing here is a better question! I have a key!"

"Open the garden door and let me in."

They stared at each other.

Mrs. Plump began to brush the dirt off her dress and said primly, "You may have a key, but I'm smart enough to know you snuck out on your mother when you should be home doing your lessons."

"If I were home doing my lessons, I wouldn't have caught you climbing over Dr. Pi's wall. That's trespassing."

"Trespassing!" Her face grew red. "I was simply watching over the neighborhood. We can't be too protective of our neighborhood's safety."

Flor shook her head and opened the door. "Come in, already."

Mrs. Plump brightened. "Did you put that outfit together all by yourself?" she asked, taking a closer look at Flor's clothes.

Flor nodded.

"Those pants are a nearly perfect black. Some shades of black are more perfect than others. Although . . ." Mrs. Plump frowned, staring at Flor's stocking feet. "Your look is ruined by the lack of a simple pair of shoes."

"I took my shoes off when I came in. I was . . . umm . . . trying to be quiet."

Mrs. Plump leaned close and whispered, "You were spying, just like me."

Flor looked away.

Mrs. Plump continued, "I don't know what you're looking for. Myself, I only wanted Dr. Pi's recipe."

"What would you do with Dr. Pi's recipe?"

"The shape of my toast is dull. Always so square. Toast that goes round and round and up and up might do wonders for my business! My ladies would find it easier to diet with toast that was entertaining."

"Do you really want his recipe?" Flor asked.

"Business is tough these days. I need every advantage."

"You can have it," she said, crawling under the table and opening the latch. She pulled out a scroll of paper and handed it to Mrs. Plump.

"What's this?"

"The recipe. And if you can understand it, you are a genius."

Mrs. Plump unrolled the paper and squinted.

"This is nothing but numbers and letters. This is nonsense," said Mrs. Plump. "This has nothing to do with pies."

"Apparently it does."

"There are no ingredients at all! Where's the sugar, fruit, butter, cream, and crust?"

"It's a mystery to me, too. Anyway, Mrs. Plump, now that you're here, I'll let you in on a secret."

Edna rolled up the scroll. She waited.

"I'm not going to tell anybody about your . . . mishap in the backyard," said Flor, "and you must swear that *you* are never going to tell a single soul about the seashell on this table."

Actually, she had goose bumps of excitement at the thought of sharing the fortune-telling shell with somebody, anybody, even the annoying Mrs. Plump.

"I have no reason to talk about a seashell," said Mrs. Plump.

"Oh, you will."

"I will?" She shook her head and said firmly, "I am Mrs. Plump, and Mrs. Plump doesn't give a hoot about seashells. Mrs. Plump cares about how we live our lives. I preach the virtues of modesty, restraint, and proper style. And speaking of style, I desperately need a change of clothes. I need a hot bath. And I could use a soothing cup of tea. Thank you for helping me. Thank you for overlooking my folly. I'd rather not leave the way I came. The front door would be preferable."

"Mrs. Plump, you can't go now."

"Dr. Pi would not be happy to find us here."

"Dr. Pi may have been kidnapped!"

Edna Plump frowned. "You have evidence of a kidnapping?"

"I'm not absolutely one hundred percent positive,

but . . . we can find out. Because, you see, this seashell can show us the future! Just you wait while I take a peek around the curve of time."

Before Mrs. Plump could laugh at her, Flor stretched on her tiptoes and stuck her head in the shell.

"Flor, get your head out of that shell. I think you have lost your mind. I'm going to bring you home to your mother myself."

"I know it looks that way," Flor said from inside the shell. "But I'm perfectly sane."

She could see Dr. Pi out on the Brooklyn Bridge doing somersaults in the air. What kind of craziness was this? With each somersault he went higher and higher, and farther and farther away.

"Flor," he somehow beamed a thought at her, "I hope you're looking around the curve of time right now, because it's midnight and I'm trying very hard to send you a message."

How did he do that? Could she do it too? She concentrated very hard herself.

"I'm here," she beamed back. Had her thought traveled

into the future? And if so, had it arrived in his head, or somebody else's head?

"I'm disappearing for a while," he beamed. "I took the fire and spiraled myself into a very tiny Dr. Pi, practically invisible. And I'm going to make myself even tinier. At the moment I'm over the Brooklyn Bridge. It's actually quite pleasant; the view of the river is sublime and the weather is perfect tonight. Now listen. I must put the fire someplace safe for now. And so the rest is up to you."

"Up to me?"

"Normally I would not ask a ten-year-old girl to help me save something as important as the Spiral. But I believe you can help me, because it was all written in a book long ago. Speaking of the book, I didn't have a chance to give it to you, so please take it from my reading room. You will learn about yourself and your family. And don't forget to use the hat!"

"That's all? You're just deserting me?"

"Have faith!" he beamed to her, but his beam grew faint. "Ride the Spiral to the very end and you will go where no one's been!"

And then he disappeared.

"Don't go," she cried out. "I'm scared!"

"Flor." Mrs. Plump tugged at her arm. "Who are you talking to?"

She squeezed and pushed and scrunched herself until she was up around another curve.

Now, however, she found nothing but darkness. It was cool and quiet except for the sound of ocean surf.

"Dr. Pi, come back! Please, show me the future!"

But the darkness sent back only silence, and she saw nothing.

She felt Mrs. Plump tugging at one foot and then the other. But Flor didn't budge. She was completely stuck.

Then she heard a sound: glass being shattered. Someone had broken the window. Or, thought Flor, *two someones*. She just knew it: The two brothers had crash-landed again. They were obviously very bad at flying.

"Crash-landed again, brother!"

"Mr. Bit, I did my best. And I think you ought to give credit where credit is due. We've arrived at the right place finally."

"We'll see. I'm Mr. Bit, still in a snit!" There was a pause. "Hello. Who are *you*?"

There was a long silence, and then a frightened voice: "I'm Mrs. Edna Plump. Why are you two dressed in ice-cream suits?"

There was another pause. "Ice-cream suits?"

"Your suits are entirely white. Thus, ice-cream suits."

"We always wear white when we travel," said Mr. It.

"Where is Pi?" asked Mr. Bit.

"You mean Dr. Pi? He has recently been kidnapped."

"How do you know that? Are you Mrs. Pi?" asked Bit.

"Mrs. Pi? You think I'm the wife of a man who feeds our entire neighborhood—"

"Delicious pies," interrupted Mr. It. "I had the pleasure of consuming one whole pie not an hour ago, at the home of Flor Bernoulli."

"*You* ate pie at Flor's house?"

"We both did," said Mr. It. "Unfortunately, we left a bad impression, as we crash-landed there, too. But we promised to pay for the broken skylight. Can you tell us where Dr. Pi is? Who kidnapped him? Since you are his wife—"

68

"I am not his wife!"

Mr. Bit said, "You're here in his home, and so clearly you are his wife."

"I'm not anybody's wife," protested Mrs. Plump. "I am quite completely on my own."

"Then are you his cleaning lady?" inquired Mr. It.

Mrs. Plump could not have been more offended. Flor could hear her sniff. "I am Edna Plump, a legend in my own time, as famous for my tea and toast as I am for my good manners and style, which you two intruders seem to lack. I shall have you know that I am famous all over Brooklyn, Manhattan, Queens, the Bronx, *and* Staten Island!"

"What is that?" said Mr. It suddenly.

"What is what?" said Mr. Bit.

"Why are there two feet sticking out of that seashell?" Flor curled her toes.

"Look at that! A seashell with feet!" said Mr. Bit. He bent over. "Hello in there! You're not in the ocean where you belong. And instead of tentacles you have toes!"

And with that Bit gave a tug on her foot.

"Ouch!" she yelped.

He gave another tug.

"Please be gentle," implored Mrs. Plump. "The poor girl's lost her mind, and on top of that she's stuck inside a shell."

"What poor girl?" asked Mr. Bit.

"Flor Bernoulli, of course," said Edna.

"I knew it! She blew it! Come out now!"

"I can't," said Flor meekly.

She could hear the twins and Mrs. Plump discussing the dilemma, and then six hands clamped onto her ankles. They yanked. They tugged. They strained and heaved. But try as they might, they could not unstick Flor.

"Maybe we should just leave her here," said Mr. Bit.

"Oh no, please don't leave me!" cried Flor.

"Enough of this," bellowed Mr. Bit. "Get ready, miss!"

And then she felt herself going up in the air, and turning upside down, and—

Crack! Flor tumbled and fell. When she sat up, she found herself on the table and the nautilus shell broken in half on either side of her.

She heaved a big sigh of relief, but then straightened her hat and glared at Mr. Bit.

"Now you've gone and done it! Now nobody will ever be able to look around the curve of time again!"

Chapter
8

A TRIP IN THE MAGIC HAT

Go ahead, make a rhyme," Flor added, seeing Mr. Bit's face fall.

"The shell that foresees the future," said Mr. It, and turned to his brother. "So it's real after all. I always thought it was just a fairy tale. And here it was right in front of us on this table in this pie shop in Brooklyn Heights, New York, U.S.A., planet Earth."

"The future is not set in stone," said Mr. Bit. "It's a gamble. It's a bet. So why be upset?" He turned to Flor. "We can all change our luck."

"I think you're stuck with your luck," said Flor.

Mr. Bit brightened at her rhyme. "Stuck with my luck?" Then he frowned. "What do you mean? The future, miss, is just a blank check. You make your own future."

"That shell showed me you two were coming for dinner," said Flor, hopping down off the table. "That's why I brought home an extra pie."

"Speaking of pies, perhaps you two men can explain this recipe," said Mrs. Plump. "This list of numbers and letters and funny marks is what Dr. Pi uses to bake his pies. I've never seen a recipe like this. How in the world am I going to know how much flour to use?"

She held out the scroll. Mr. Bit unrolled it and squinted, muttering to himself and drawing shapes in the air. Finally he looked up with a satisfied smile. "Yeee-eees sireee! This is the math equation for the Spiral. This is what makes your friend's pies special. The Spiral. Which gets us back to the point. Where is he?"

"Tell them, dear," said Mrs. Plump.

Flor shook her head. "No way."

Mrs. Plump squeezed her hand and said firmly, "Flor,

tell him about the kidnappers, so these two men can catch them and bring them to justice."

"The kidnappers?"

"The awful kidnappers who took Dr. Pi," Mrs. Plump emphasized. "It's a miracle we managed to escape at all!"

"Oh, *those* awful kidnappers. They disappeared upstairs," Flor said.

"And out the window," added Mrs. Plump.

"They were holding him upside down by his feet out the window," said Flor. "And then they jumped. But instead of falling down, they fell up."

The brothers eyed her suspiciously.

"Not many people can fall up when they fall down," said Mr. Bit.

"It's a rare talent," agreed Mr. It. "I only know of one such person with that ability, and he's our cousin. I don't see what our cousin would be doing here. He's quite happy on his star."

"These men said that Dr. Pi would never see his shop again," Mrs. Plump continued, enjoying her story as she made it up. Of course, making up stories was a questionable moral act, except when discovered trespassing by other trespassers.

"They are going to put the fire out once and for all," Flor added.

"Put out the fire?" yelped Mr. Bit.

"That's right," said Mrs. Plump, warming to the thought. "No more pies. Ever again. Of course, I will be here to comfort the entire neighborhood while we all mourn."

"I am done for," said Mr. It suddenly in a small voice. He covered his eyes with his hands. Then he slid slowly down the wall until he was sitting on the floor.

Mr. Bit crouched down beside his brother.

"How are you feeling?"

Mr. It shook his head. "Not too swift."

"We have at least thirty-six hours left. And maybe more. Can you make it?"

"I don't know."

Mr. Bit stood up. "Flor and you, Mrs. Not-His-Wife and Not-His-Cleaning-Lady, whoever you are, we are in a desperate emergency. Please show us exactly where those kidnappers went."

And so the four of them traipsed up two flights of stairs, Mrs. Plump leading the way, head high as if she had nothing to fear and was determined only to pursue justice. Flor followed in her stocking feet, thinking, *This is a total disaster.* And the twin brothers brought up the rear, taking steps together, as if they were practicing to be in a marching band.

When they got to the top landing there was a long hall with five doors, all of them shut.

Flor had never been upstairs.

"The key is in my hat, of course," she said to the others, unzipping the secret compartment.

She took a few hesitant steps.

"Hurry, miss," urged Mr. Bit.

"You can call me Flor," she said. "That's my name, not miss."

"Of course, Flor," Mr. It said softly. "Please hurry."

"Mr. It, why are you shivering?" she asked, for he had wrapped his arms around himself, and his teeth were chattering.

"He's cold, why else would he shiver?" answered Mr. Bit,

putting an arm around his brother. "Which door?"

Well, thought Flor, if she was going to be caught, now was as good a time as any. She walked boldly up to the third door and turned the key in the lock.

The door swung open with a loud creak.

The room was black as a buried cave, and warm as summer. She could feel a thick carpet under her feet and smell the odor of old leather and tobacco. She felt for the wall and took slow steps in the dark.

"Ouch!" said Mr. Bit. "I hit a couch! Can't see a thing."

"I'm trying to find a light," said Flor. "This is Dr. Pi's reading room. He described it to me many times," she murmured as her hand slowly moved across the top of a table. It closed on a gooseneck lamp. She ran her fingers up the metal curve of the lamp, found a chain, and pulled.

Soft light bathed the room. She was standing in front of Dr. Pi's leather recliner. On the little table was a plate of untouched blueberry pie. And the book he'd been reading, a small old book with a peeling calfskin cover, left open on the seat of the chair. Was this *the* book? She turned it over to look at the title.

The History of the Bernoulli Family from the Seventeenth Century Until Present Times. Flor slid the book into the pocket of her pants. At the window were heavy velvet curtains that Mr. Bit was, at this very moment, pulling open.

"The window is shut," said Mr. Bit. He tried to heave it open. "And it's locked! I am shocked!" Mr. Bit's two blond eyebrows lifted up almost as high as his hairline.

And that was when Flor spun around and began to run. Mrs. Plump ran after her. At the top of the stairs, Flor skidded to a stop. Dr. Pi's hat had lifted itself off her head and began to whirr and then started bouncing down the steps. As the hat bobbed and bounced it turned over on itself and, with each turn, got bigger.

And bigger.

Until it stopped on the second-floor landing.

"Let me go after them!" she heard Mr. Bit arguing with his brother. "You need the fire."

"I've caught a bad chill," she heard Mr. It say.

"You're burning the last of your fire."

"I think I am. You always said I was the lucky one, but it looks like the opposite is true."

"Your luck is stuck, that's all. You're down to embers now. You must rest somehow. Use your fire to stay alive."

"We've never been apart," Mr. It reminded his twin. "Not for a single minute."

"Mr. Bit and Mr. It," he agreed. "We're a pair like no other, brother and brother."

Mr. It sighed and apparently sat down. "Ahhh," he said. "I would like a nap. . . ."

Oh no, thought Flor. *Mr. It is sick, but with what?*

There was no time to wonder about it. Flor grabbed Mrs. Plump's hand and said, "Follow me! And do whatever I do!"

Halfway down the stairs, she took a running leap, aiming straight for the hat. She fell right in.

"Mrs. Plump!" she called. "Jump!"

There was a loud wail. "I can't jump, I have never jumped, a lady never jumps, and I'm a lady and I— *eeeeeek*—that crazy Mr. Bit—I—"

And the next thing she knew, Mrs. Plump had leaped straight into the hat. She practically landed on her head. But the hat was soft and she wasn't hurt.

Flor heard Mr. Bit calling back to his brother. "They've trapped themselves in a hat! I'm going after them!"

"What do we do now, Flor?" whispered Mrs. Plump, who was quivering with terror. Her dress was now torn down both sides, and her sleeves hung loose like two black rags.

"Poor Mrs. Plump," said Flor. "It hasn't been a very good night, has it?"

"In all my life I've never had a night as awful as this."

"Let's try and roll the hat down the next flight of stairs. Either it will get bigger than it is now, or it will get much smaller."

They could hear Mr. Bit marching down the stairs, still laughing to himself because they'd stupidly trapped themselves in a hat.

"Ready or not, here I come!" boomed Mr. Bit, with both hands on the rim and one leg over it. "I'm climbing in!"

"Mrs. Plump, it's now or never!" shouted Flor.

And together, Flor Bernoulli from Brooklyn Heights, New York, and Mrs. Edna Plump, proprietor of the famous Tea and Toast shop, gave the hat of hats a tremendous shove.

Chapter
9

A STAIRWAY COMES TO THE RESCUE

It's one thing, thought Flor, to take a bumpy, galumphy spin through space in a hat that keeps getting bigger and bigger. . . . oh sure, it's one thing to have Mrs. Edna Plump (a lady who, only hours ago, you totally hated) practically strangle you with a grip of pure terror as you both tumble and fall . . . and to hear her cry, "I'm seasick! My head is going in three different directions! Stop this hat!" . . . and, sure, it's one thing to realize that the hat has left Dr. Pi's shop and must be rising over the rooftops because you can hear traffic, and then ocean surf, and then the roar of airplanes, and then . . . no sound at all . . . except the sound of night and space. . . .

And it is another thing, Flor went on thinking, another thing entirely to take this trip with Mr. Bit, who lurched into the hat in the nick of time and now with every turn tumbles past you, and each time he passes, shouts out some absurd rhyme:

"Your navigation skills are an atrocity!" he says as he falls through space.

"This hat has no absolute viscosity!" he says the next time he seems to fly past.

"The Spiral is not just some curiosity!"

And it's one thing, thought Flor, to be lost in the space of an expanding hat, and another to feel the hat start to spin in the opposite direction, and get *smaller* with each turn. You can't help but wonder if the hat gets too small, what will happen to the three people squeezed inside it?

"It's freezing in this crazy hat," moaned Mrs. Plump.

"I think we're over the ocean," said Flor.

"Good guess, miss," shouted Mr. Bit as he somersaulted past her, his skinny arms flung out. He seemed to be enjoying himself. "I'll be back in a moment, won't I!"

"He's going nowhere fast," Flor muttered.

And they spun smaller and smaller, so that pretty soon their arms were touching, and they were tumbling together like three sticks in a matchbox.

"We're packed in pretty tight tonight!" Mr. Bit said as his face swam up near Flor's. "Am I right?"

Flor said nothing. Mr. Bit looked irritated.

"No time for a rhyme?" He pouted.

Flor turned away from him.

"Why did I ever climb over Dr. Pi's wall?" Mrs. Plump was wailing softly to herself. "It was wrong, wrong, wrong, to break in on anyone, and I suppose I deserve this awful punishment. I could be at home planning my ladies' diets and instead I'm trapped in a hat with a bossy ten-year-old girl and a man who is *so* odd you can see through him to the other side!"

Bump. Galumph. Oof! Smaller and smaller still.

"Ouch!" yelped Flor. "Stop elbowing me, Mr. Bit!"

"I need space for my elbows. And you seem to be intruding on my space."

Flor sighed. "There's no space left."

"You put us into the hat, miss, and it's up to you to get us out of the hat," said Mr. Bit.

"Call me Flor, not miss! And how the heck am I supposed to get us out? I'm not really sure how we got *in*."

"Well, for starters," said Mr. Bit, whose elbows were now pushed so tight they seemed to be halfway inside his body, "you might decide to open this zipper here. Who knows what we'd find inside."

She had completely forgotten about the zipper and the magic staircase. Instantly she opened it and a single step popped out, and naturally, she put her feet on it, and naturally, Mrs. Plump followed her.

"There's no room for you," she said to Mr. Bit.

"Oh yes there is!" he said, lifting one long leg and then the other until he was standing in his white sneakers on Flor's shoulders.

"How rude!" said Mrs. Plump. "He doesn't have even a morsel of manners."

"Actually, he's as light as a feather. I can't feel him at all," said Flor.

And then the step swiveled and the three of them found themselves outside the hat.

Chapter
10

THEY FIND THEMSELVES IN A LIGHTHOUSE

It was night, but such a night as Flor had never known. A night of soft rain and blankets of purple mist and the odor of hot sand. Above her was a sky, but such a sky Flor had never seen before. It was stuffed to bursting with stars—they would surely spill onto her head like snow at any moment. And it was warm, a clean, sweet, relaxing warmth. Oh, how far, far from home she must be.

The famous hat had vanished, and the step had gone with it. Instead there were stairs. Flor was standing at the top of a huge swirling stone staircase: stairs and stairs that went round and round and down and down, as far as the eye could see.

"Wow," breathed Flor. "I just can't . . . even . . . describe it."

"From the pictures I've seen in travel books," said Mrs. Plump, "I would say we've landed in a lighthouse. A very old one."

"An old lighthouse," whispered Flor. "To light the way for sailing ships at sea. Do you really think so?"

"I'll tell you exactly where we are," said Mr. Bit, reaching into his pocket and withdrawing a gizmo with spikes and curves sticking out. He swung it around and pushed some buttons. "I'm an expert navigator, you know. Better than my twin brother, who always crashes through black holes. Let's see. Latitude about forty-six degrees . . . hmmm . . . looks like we are on an island called the Île de Ré. And we are very specifically at the top of the Lighthouse of the Whales, at the top of a spiral staircase of two hundred and fifty-seven steps."

"Where is the island, pray tell?" murmured Mrs. Plump.

"Off the coast of France."

"France? Are we near Paris?" whispered Flor.

"Not too far, at least by car," said Mr. Bit, frowning at her. "Why?"

"Oh, no reason at all," said Flor. But she already knew in her heart of hearts: She was going to meet her father after all! Why else would the magic hat have taken her to France? Her dad was asleep in a bed somewhere in Paris, and she was on her way to him.

"Mr. Bit, what time is it?" she asked very politely. "I hope you notice I just rhymed," she added even more politely.

"A little after four in the morning, French time," he replied. He looked at her suspiciously. "Why are you being so nice?"

"Can we get to Paris by breakfast?"

"What is in Paris?"

"An airplane flight, of course," said Flor quickly. "I don't see the hat anywhere. It seems to have completely deserted us. I hope it shows up again, but it looks like the only way out is down these stairs and then on to Paris and home."

"I would prefer if your hat had taken us to a comfortable bed!" Mrs. Plump said. "This lighthouse is much too high and narrow. Every time I look at that staircase I lose my balance. In fact, I believe I am about to throw up."

How she was going to find her father in all of Paris, Flor had no idea. She knew many facts about the city, though, because she'd looked them up online. There were over two million people. There were eight thousand restaurants. There were two thousand hotels. *I'll think about all that when I get there,* she promised herself.

"First we find Pi," said Mr. Bit.

"Dr. Pi never said anything to me about a lighthouse in France." Flor shook her head. "I just . . . don't get the feeling . . . that he's here. Honestly."

Mr. Bit looked terribly upset. Flor was starting to feel sorry for him, and guilty about the trick she and Mrs. Plump had played on the brothers.

"I have a confession to make," Flor burst out, "but you must promise me you won't get mad."

"I promise, but I'm lying."

"Mr. Bit!" she pleaded.

He shrugged helplessly. "I'm trying, I'm trying. But I might get mad."

"Well then, promise me you won't think too badly of me."

He scowled. "I promise."

"I know where Dr. Pi is."

She expected him to be angry with her, but surprisingly, he was calm. "Where?"

"He's back in New York, spinning over the Brooklyn Bridge, actually."

Mr. Bit did not seem surprised to hear it. "So we came all this way for nothing?"

"The hat flew us here—not me!"

"You should learn to drive a hat better."

"Don't you wonder why he's spinning?" she couldn't help asking, hoping Mr. Bit might enlighten her.

Mr. Bit shrugged. "I suspect he's spinning himself smaller and smaller, and higher and higher until he and the fire are so little they can pop through a hole into another dimension. And then he can hide the fire from me. Right?"

"Well, I . . . suppose."

He squinted at her.

"You don't have the faintest clue what I'm talking

about," he said. "Not the faintest clue. Do you? Do you? You don't understand the least little bit. The least little *Bit*," he repeated emphatically.

"It's true," she admitted. "It all sounds crazy to me. But if we can get to Paris and then get home, I'll ask Dr. Pi to help your brother."

"Hmmm," he said, frowning.

"It's just that stealing the fire is not . . . well . . . it's just not an option. All the spirals in the world would go flat."

"I know. They would just turn into numbers. There would be no life left in them at all. That's what will happen to my brother, too," said Mr. Bit dejectedly.

Flor shook her head. "I don't understand. How can a spiral go flat? How can something real turn into numbers?"

"A man is a man," agreed Mrs. Plump. "A man is not math."

"We are all numbers. The whole universe is numbers," said Mr. Bit. "You just can't see the numbers, so you think they aren't there. What do I care? My brother will die without the fire. And he's my only brother and all that I have."

All three of them were silent, staring down the 257 steps below them.

"Well?" asked Flor.

"Well," sighed Mrs. Plump.

"Very well," agreed Mr. Bit.

And so they dusted off their clothes and began the long, slow descent. One after another, their hands firmly holding the railing so as not to get dizzy, they went round and round and down and down while the skinny, see-through fellow from outer space told the story of the Brothers Bit and It and how numbers turn into men.

Chapter
11

THE BROTHERS BIT AND IT

I t's a strange, strange place in outer space," said Mr. Bit, his metallic voice clanging loudly down the stairwell. "Your Earth is twenty-four trillion miles away from the nearest star. Well, guess where we are? We are eight times farther away than that. Yes, it's a strange, strange place in outer space."

One, two, three. Down the steps they went. Mr. Bit shook his head, as if he were remembering the yawning cavern of space he'd flown through with his brother.

"Our planet is called Dog."

"Dog?" echoed Flor, giggling.

Mr. Bit shrugged. "That's short for Doggerel."

"Planet Doggerel," murmured Mrs. Plump. "That's exceedingly odd."

"Why? What is doggerel?" asked Flor.

"Poetry that's fit for a dog, dear," said Mrs. Plump. "Trite little rhymes. You know—roses are red, violets are blue."

"Spirals are round, circles are too," said Mr. Bit. "On Planet Dog, we start out as numbers and turn into people. Parents mix and match the numbers they want, and the numbers determine all that you will be. From the hair on your head to your personality. And then they go to the fire-breather, who blows fire into the numbers."

He paused. They waited expectantly.

"My parents wanted two boys. But they were poor and only had enough fire for one. So they copied my numbers, to make twins, and asked the fire-breather to blow half into each. But the fire-breather made a mistake. He blew almost all the fire into Mr. It and a mere lick of flame into Mr. Bit. That's why Mr. It looks real and I don't. Mr. It is very close to complete, while I am sort of between a number and a person."

"Is that why you never have an appetite?"

"Why, certainly!"

"And that's why we can see through you to the other side?" added Mrs. Plump.

"Without a doubt!" Suddenly Mr. Bit looked dejected. "The experiment failed. I don't need much fire to survive. I'm barely here as it is. But my brother is so close to complete he has burned too much fire trying to live. He'd be better off if he could be like me. And so his fire is going out."

"What will happen?" whispered Flor.

"My brother will turn back into numbers and disappear to life as we know it unless we find fire somewhere, fast."

"Are you serious? He's going to die?"

Mr. Bit shook his head. "Not exactly. He will exist, but only as numbers. He won't be able to eat or talk or laugh or walk or love."

"But can't they give him just a little extra fire?"

"On Planet Dog, it's against the law. If you steal fire and get caught you are sent to the fire-sucker, who sucks all the fire right out of you. And then of course, you turn back into numbers. You can't cheat fate."

"And you came all this way for Dr. Pi's fire?"

"I did the math. The closest fire to Planet Dog was in Brooklyn, New York, at the Sky-High Pie Shop. We had to try, can't let him die! I have no idea why we landed at your doorstep instead. My brother navigates only slightly better than you drive a hat."

"I'm starting to get the picture."

"Is a pie worth more than my brother's life?"

"Certainly not!" said Edna Plump firmly. "Ban those pies! Off with their heads, and off with their spirals! I'm happy to help in any way I can."

"Dr. Pi protects the Spiral for the *whole universe*," said Flor. "But I wonder who made Dr. Pi the Keeper of the Spiral? Maybe that person could help us. We've got to find some extra fire somewhere, that's for sure." She sighed. "Extra fire, extra fire. We need to find some extra fire."

Mr. Bit glared at her. "Are you making fun of me?"

"Not at all."

"You're not?"

"I swear I'm not."

"How can I be sure?"

"I just swore on it!"

He frowned. "I am never sure if people mean what they say. A number is true and simple and clear. Three doesn't pretend that it's really four. Seven doesn't act like six. But I don't know why, people lie."

"We lie so we won't get punished," said Flor. "Or we lie to get something we want. Or we even lie to impress somebody else." She had just lied to her own mother. Her Chinese food had probably been delivered by now, and her mom must have discovered that she was missing.

"I'm Mr. Bit, I just don't fit. And why do people say yes when they mean no? Can anyone say so?"

"It's just the way people are," Mrs. Plump chimed in. "I hate it too. They contradict themselves. I can hardly find a lady who will stay on a diet. She gets up in the morning, full of hope and resolve. All day long she eats a proper diet and snacks only on tea and toast. She's so virtuous! By dinnertime, she's opening a box of fudge."

"So?" said Mr. Bit. "Why shouldn't she snack on fudge?"

"Because she promised not to!"

"And why did she make a promise she didn't want to keep?"

"Because she wants to be slim!"

Mr. Bit shook his head. "Well, there you go. Numbers are never so contradictory."

"Mr. Bit, I don't understand how people can start out as numbers," said Flor. "That part seems really strange."

Mr. Bit picked a fleck of dirt off his white sleeve. "I can't explain it to a child."

"Please," said Flor. She could hardly believe her own voice. She was pleading to be taught math. *Math.*

"Numbers are lovely."

"I don't see how a number can be *lovely*."

"*Lovely* is a black dinner dress," said Edna Plump.

"Let me ask you a question. Do you think your world got here by chance?" asked Mr. Bit.

"I have no idea," admitted Flor.

"No idea?"

"No idea," she said firmly.

He was quiet. He seemed stumped. Then suddenly he brightened. "Your Spiral. Have you ever really noticed it?"

"Umm . . . not until today, actually, no."

"Your Spiral is in seashells."

"I know. Like the one you broke."

"And snail shells."

"Really?"

"And pine cones."

"From pine trees?"

"Pine cones from pine trees. Exactly. Spiderwebs. Galaxies. It's all the Spiral. Big or small, stars or ears, the Spiral is here and there and everywhere and always follows the same exact math."

"Are you serious?"

Mr. Bit crossed his arms and said nothing.

"You mean that—umm—that formula Dr. Pi bakes his pies from—that crazy equation he calls a recipe—is in all this stuff—" She stopped and shook her head. "Wow. It's all linked, but I still don't understand how."

"Look," he said, "one plus two equals three. Right?"

She nodded.

"We understand that," said Mrs. Plump. "One crazy fellow from outer space plus two fine females from Brooklyn equals three people stuck in a lighthouse."

"That's right," he laughed. "And one pie plus two pies equals three pies. One finger plus two fingers equals three fingers. One plus two equals three. You see? The math never changes."

"Okay," said Flor. "So?"

"The Spiral has a math formula too. It's just way too complex for a girl like you. And," he added in a chiding tone, "that's a fact and there's nothing you can do."

"I don't care if I don't understand it. Tell me about it," she said. "Anyway, that formula was what Dr. Pi called his recipe."

"Right. He was baking pies shaped like spirals."

"But I still don't see how numbers turn into people."

"That's what the fire-breather does!" Mr. Bit spluttered, frustrated. "You don't understand?"

"Nope, not at all."

"He breathes fire into the math."

They looked at him and slowly shook their heads.

"What is he talking about?" murmured Edna Plump. "Is he saying somebody breathes fire into one plus two equals three?"

"I have no idea," admitted Flor.

Mr. Bit stamped his foot. "I will quote. 'In order to understand the universe, you must know the language in which it is written. And that language is mathematics.' Who said that? Galileo Galilei. Don't you see? No, you don't. Well, you two go on alone. I'm going back to Brooklyn."

"You can't go back to Brooklyn. We've lost the magic hat!"

"I don't need a silly hat. I can just dispense with that. Why, I'll just calculate the headwinds and tailwinds, which is easy for me but impossible for you, and then spread my arms and let the wind carry me home. Remember, I hardly weigh anything. I can blow across the ocean like a little bird."

"And then what?" demanded Flor, pretending she wasn't scared to death. She needed Mr. Bit to help her get to Paris. She couldn't miss the chance to finally see her dad again. "You don't even know where Dr. Pi is hiding."

"I've got to save my brother. And I am *certain* you will *never* take me to Pi," he said. "You'd rather let my brother die, and I am not dumb enough to fall for *that*."

And he turned around and started to walk up the stairs instead of down.

Chapter
12

DR. PI COMES BACK

A fellow who is barely there, a fellow such as Mr. Bit, can fly up stairways lickety-split. Like a grasshopper he skipped ever higher, round and round and up and up, on his way to the top of the lighthouse.

Flor scrambled up the stairs after him. Behind her, Edna Plump protested.

"You know I can't run up the stairs in these heels!"

Flor turned around. "Then take them off."

"They cost a fortune!"

She gave Edna Plump a look.

"My darling shoes . . . good-bye, my darlings, forever."

She tossed both shoes down the immense stairwell. *Plunk! Kerplunk!* Now in her stocking feet, the very prim and proper Edna Plump ran up the lighthouse stairs as fast as she could.

When they reached the top, they found Mr. Bit sitting against the stone wall, legs stretched out and casually crossed at the ankles. He held his flashing gizmo in his hands, and was tapping buttons and humming a song to himself.

I'm Mr. Bit, I just don't fit.
Sometimes I fly into a snit.
And then I throw a hissy fit.
My brother's name is Mr. It.
Truth is we're a perfect fit.
He's all I have, my Mr. It.
I really cannot babysit
That wayward girl, and so I quit.
My brother's life is ALL. That's it!

Wayward girl? thought Flor. She almost turned around and marched back down the stairs. But where would she go?

"The fact is, I'm stuck," she said out loud.

"What?" Mr. Bit looked up. "Oh." His face fell. "You two."

"We three," said Flor. "You jumped into the hat with us, and you can't abandon us now. You're stuck too."

Mr. Bit leaped to his feet. "My math tells me a strong headwind is coming just ahead of a storm in ten minutes. Sorry I can't stay to discuss one, two, or three. I'm going to jump when the wind gusts."

"And fall a long way!" Flor shot back.

"I won't fall at all. I have wings. I'm such a clever Mr. Bit! You see, I brought my travel kit."

He pulled a small green box out of his pocket, opened it, unfolded a pair of wings, and strapped them on. They were curved on top and flat underneath. He craned his neck upward and rolled his shoulders back, then strolled out onto the balcony that encircled the top of the lighthouse. Like a grasshopper, he lifted one long leg and then the other onto the sturdy stone parapet.

Mrs. Plump said in a firm voice, "If anybody thinks I

am following Mr. Doggerel Nitwit onto that parapet and making a suicide jump, they have another think coming. That means you, Flor Bernoulli. Don't you dare tell me to leap to my death."

"Mrs. Plump, do you believe he can actually fly with those flimsy wings?" Flor taunted. Mr. Bit was doing his best to ignore her. "They seem to be made of such thin plastic."

"He may be able to fly off this island," said Mrs. Plump firmly, "but he can't fly across the ocean. He'll fall into the water a few miles out. Then he'll have to swim ashore."

"If he *knows* how to swim," said Flor. "Since they suck fire on Planet Doggerel, they're probably terrified of water. He'll probably melt like the Wicked Witch of the West as soon as he falls into the sea."

"Meanwhile," sighed Edna, "you and I will be spending half the day climbing down those dreadful stairs in our bare feet."

"Look on the bright side, your shoes are down there somewhere."

"Seven more minutes until takeoff," Mr. Bit said loudly. "And no, I won't fall! And no, I won't melt!"

Flor couldn't help giggling. He really did look funny, standing on the parapet in his white suit, skinny as a beanpole, with his fake wings.

"Six minutes!" Mr. Bit called out.

"Mrs. Plump, did you *feel* that?"

"Did I feel *what?*" said Mrs. Plump, pushing her hair back as it blew across her face.

"Big wind's a-comin'," boomed Mr. Bit. "Don't stall, it'll get us all! Five minutes to countdown!"

"It's just like he predicted," Flor whispered.

The sky had darkened. Black clouds skidded toward them. A sharp, stinging rain spattered their faces.

"Three minutes and I'll be flying! Three minutes and you'll be crying!"

"You're not going without me!" said Flor, and threw her arms around his ankles, hugging them tightly.

"Let go!" Mr. Bit slapped her head with his plastic wing.

"Wherever you're going, I'm going too!"

"You aren't, either!" Mrs. Plump shouted. "They'll blame *me* for letting you fall to your death."

"Get off my legs!" But Mr. Bit saw it was no good. Flor had a grip as tight as lobster claws. "All right, then, climb onto my back, but do it *now*. Right *now*. Nobody can fly with a ten-year-old girl hanging off their feet. The aerodynamics are a disaster, and we'll crash as soon as we lift off."

Without further ado, Flor scrambled up onto the parapet and onto his back. It was like holding on to a pole made of marshmallows.

"Ten, nine, eight, seven, six . . . Are you ready?"

"As ready as I'll ever be!"

Just then the wind gusted and howled, as if some great god in the sky was trying to blow the entire island out to sea, and Mr. Bit spread his wings and jumped into the air.

"What a balmy breeze!"

"Wow! I'm flying in France just like a bird!" said Flor.

Mr. Bit tilted his left wing down and his right wing up, and they turned smoothly west, out to sea. They passed right in front of Edna Plump, who hadn't moved from her spot. Both hands were splayed on her cheeks and her mouth was open so wide you could practically see down to her stomach.

Below, the water churned. Not far off, a flock of gulls soared, and for a moment Flor completely forgot to be scared, because it was all so beautiful—the stormy sky and the white foam flickering on the water and the infinite unfolding space all around her.

"What if the wind stops and we fall into the ice-cold ocean? Can we really coast on the wind all the way to Brooklyn? And won't it take several days?" she wondered.

But she never got a chance to find out. At that moment a ball of red and blue in the sky caught her attention.

It was headed straight toward them.

It was turning and turning.

It was the magic hat!

Before she could blink, the hat was huge and right up against them, and she and Mr. Bit flew into its mouth. Then it stopped, spun in the opposite direction, and landed over Mrs. Plump. The hat tilted until Mr. Bit grabbed her by the arm and pulled her in. And then they were off again.

"So, Flor," a familiar, friendly voice said. "Do you know yet what breathes fire into the equations?"

"Dr. Pi!"

If she could have, Flor would have kissed his shiny, bald head. She was so glad to see him. But they were tumbling in the spinning hat.

"How did you get here? Is Mr. It still alive? Where are we going?" she called as she fell past him.

"Why, Paris, of course," he called back to her. "But before we arrive, which should be very soon, you have a bit of reading to catch up on. Did you look up your family history in the book?"

She had completely forgotten about the book in her pocket.

"Who cares about family histories? What about my brother?" asked Mr. Bit anxiously.

"He's weak, but still alive. I think we have time for Flor to visit her dad in Paris, *and* get back to help Mr. It."

"Visit her *dad*?" exclaimed Mrs. Plump. "Why should the rest of us tag along to see a man who deserted his own child? He's clearly a deadbeat."

"He'll totally regret leaving once he sees me," Flor said sharply. "Either he'll beg me to live in France or he'll come back to Brooklyn. It'll be perfect. Maybe he'll even remarry my mother!"

"Your mother? What about my brother? What about the fire?" Mr. Bit interjected again. "I need to get back to Brooklyn, not dawdle in Paris."

"You and I should have a talk about that," said Dr. Pi. "You know very well I'd be breaking *the* law if I gave fire to your brother. A much bigger law than on planet Earth— or Planet Dog, for that matter. A universal law."

"But I can't let my brother die."

"No," said Dr. Pi. "You can't. And neither can I."

"So what do we do?" asked Flor. "We have to save the Spiral and save Mr. It. And we can't do one without destroying the other."

"We're stuck, we're stuck, it's lousy luck," Mr. Bit said, obviously upset. "We're stuck between a rock and a rock."

"A rock and a hard place," said Flor.

"A rock and a rock," Mr. Bit repeated.

"But we have an advantage," Dr. Pi said. "Right here with us. Her name is Flor Bernoulli."

Chapter
13

IT'S A FAMILY AFFAIR

Flor had too many questions for Dr. Pi. She wanted to know: Where was the fire? What kept it burning? How did fire get into spirals? How did numbers turn into people? Why did he decide to spin over the Brooklyn Bridge, and how did he protect the fire all these years? Why had the magic hat disappeared from France, reappeared in Brooklyn, and taken him back to France? And when had he realized that Mr. Bit and Mr. It were not his mortal enemies—just two desperate men whizzing through the universe in search of fire?

"I don't have time to answer so many questions!" Dr. Pi laughed, reading her mind as usual. "I can tell you I spun the fire down into a tiny dot that nobody can see and stuck it in another dimension for now."

"Thought so," grumbled Mr. Bit.

"It can't stay there forever. I'll have to go get it soon. Fire likes to burn. It likes to leap and lick and spark. It likes to keep the universe turning. As for the hat," Dr. Pi continued, "it has a mind of its own. It's just taken us to the Rue de Seine, one of the oldest streets in Paris. It's seven in the morning in France. I believe your father takes his coffee about two hours from now at a bistro called La Palette a few blocks from here."

"La Palette?" echoed Flor.

It was too good to be true. In a few hours her life would finally become whole. She would no longer be the kid at school who couldn't remember what her dad's voice sounded like. The one who, every birthday, hoped for some little present from Paris that never arrived. The girl walking around with a craterlike hole in her life, as if some giant fist in the sky had scooped out the part of life called "Dad" and left nothing in its place. The worst times were summer barbecues at friends' houses, since somebody's dad was always flipping burgers on the grill in the backyard and pretending to play air guitar at the same time, and then beaming at his own daughter like he had never laid eyes on such a wondrous creature in his life. Was there some reason every single classmate of hers had lucked out with a proper father—even the ones whose parents were divorced—and she had to get the one dad who flew off to another part of the world when she was a baby? She had always known she was going to make it right someday. . . .

Dr. Pi's voice interrupted her reverie. "Flor—let me just ask—are you sure you want to meet him like this? He isn't exactly prepared for your visit."

"Are you kidding?"

He sighed. "Just remember, the future doesn't always match up with our wishes. Sometimes the future knows where we're going even when we have plans to go somewhere else."

"I'm ready for my future," Flor said confidently.

"Well, until the *future* arrives, we've got oodles of time to go window-shopping and I can get some new shoes and a new dress and see the finest French fashions," said Mrs. Plump. "What do you think, Flor? You're a little bundle of fashion yourself. Shall we go together and gape at the storefronts? My ladies will be begging to hear what Parisians are wearing."

"I'd love to, but I've got reading to do," said Flor, opening Dr. Pi's small, leather-bound book.

Mrs. Plump's face fell and her lip began to quiver. "Flor, I can't be seen in a Paris café looking like a raga-muffin with no shoes. And I certainly can't go shopping with these two men. You must come with me."

"But I can't," protested Flor. "Here, take my lace scarf and my cape. I don't need them, and they'll dress you up beautifully. I admit it's not perfect, but for now it will have to do." Then she turned to the book. "This is about my family, can you believe it? A whole book about people who had the same last name as me. They handed down the power of the Spiral, and it's part of my destiny," she went on, not quite sure what she meant, but it sounded impressive. Dr. Pi nodded. "My dad knows all about this. My dad draws spirals in every artwork he makes. I overheard Mom saying so right before I snuck out."

Edna Plump reached for the book, but not before Mr. Bit could snatch it.

"Let *me* see that. *I'm* the math whiz. I'll tell you if your ancestors were fakers or not."

He opened the little book, turned to the first chapter, and began to read out loud.

"'*The History of the Bernoulli Family from the Seventeenth Century Until Present Times.*'" He paused. "'The Bernoullis were a Swiss family that dominated mathematics in the seventeenth and eighteenth centuries. Like a dynasty of kings, the Bernoullis were the royalty of math. They made so many discoveries that without them, math as we know it today simply would not exist. The first generation included Jakob the first and his brother Johann the first. The next generation included Jakob's nephew Nicolaus the first and Johann's three sons, Nicolaus the second, Daniel, and Johann the second. Finally, the third generation included Johann the third and Jakob the second.'"

"That's *my* family?"

Mr. Bit nodded. "Apparently. Let me see what they invented and discovered." He flipped ahead through the chapters. "Not bad, not bad," he said to himself. "Quite. Yes! Look at that. That's fantastic!"

"Tell me about them!" insisted Flor.

Mr. Bit looked up. "You do come from a superior line," he admitted. "Which you really don't deserve, considering that you can't even fly a hat in a straight line, in spite of the fact that apparently your ancestor, Daniel Bernoulli, explained the principle behind flight."

Flor frowned. "What principle is that?"

Mr. Bit shrugged. "Air moves faster over the top of the wing than the bottom, if the top is curved properly. And the slower air underneath has higher pressure. So it holds the bird up! Just like my fake wings. In any case, your ancestors understood calculus and curves, principles and polarities. On Planet Dog they would be given prizes."

"Tell me about the Spiral, please."

"The Spiral." He thumbed through the book. "Here it is. Chapter Six. It was a favorite of your ancestor Jakob the first. In the year 1692 he named it the *spira mirabilis*."

"Which means?"

"'Miraculous spiral,'" said Dr. Pi. "Remember how I told you that no matter how small or big, the Spiral's proportions always stay the same?"

"I remember," said Flor. She could hardly believe how much had happened since this afternoon. Not even a whole day had passed, and her entire life had turned upside down. *Upside down and round and round*, she thought, *just like a spiral*.

"It grows larger without ever changing its shape," he continued. "That's a beautiful thing. Sort of miraculous, I'd say."

"Not as miraculous as a rectangle with its beautiful and deeply simple corners!" said Mr. Bit. He went back to the book. "Eh . . . what is this? *Eadem mutata resurgo semperdem*."

"Latin," said Dr. Pi. "Before Jakob died, he asked that those words be inscribed on his gravestone, along with an engraving of the Spiral."

"What do they mean?" asked Flor.

"'I shall arise again the same, though changed. Always.'"

"If he put it on his grave it must mean something important, but I can't imagine what that is."

Dr. Pi thought for a moment. "He was trying to describe the Spiral. Jakob understood that we are all like the Spiral. Though we change and grow and learn through life, something deep in us remains the same. Just like the Spiral, which gets bigger and bigger, but never changes its proportions. And so, we too are always changed, and ever the same."

"This book has no ending," Mr. Bit announced. "The last chapter has twenty completely blank pages."

"The last chapter has not been written yet," said Dr. Pi.

Mr. Bit looked straight at Flor. "Believe it or not, this chapter has *your* name on it."

He handed the book to her.

"I can't believe it. There's my name, right there. Such fancy script! And my birthday. And my address. But there's nothing else about me. Nothing at all!"

"It's very simple. You haven't done anything important yet," Mr. Bit said.

Flor turned to Dr. Pi. "Didn't you tell me I have a destiny? I'm a Bernoulli, you said."

"It could be *your* *c*hapter will turn out to be the most interesting one of all," he answered.

"The magic hat that flew us to that staircase in France," Flor said slowly. "It didn't do that by chance, did it?"

"Very little happens just by chance," said Dr. Pi. "How did you like that staircase, by the way?"

"I've never seen anything so . . . grand. It made me dizzy."

"You see," said Dr. Pi. "We must experience things ourselves. And now aren't you amazed that the same spiral shape is inside your ear?"

She nodded. "Mr. Bit says you can write out the same math formula for both."

"Right." Dr. Pi beamed at her.

"I have another question."

"Shoot."

"Is it meant to be—am I meant to meet my dad now?"

"It seems so. If only because you want it so much."

"I don't see *how* this girl is going to save my brother," said Mr. Bit. "She's just a *girl,* and with so many questions, how can she have any answers?"

Flor turned to Mr. Bit. "I have no idea. I promise I won't take very long with my dad, and we'll get back with hours to spare and figure out how to save Mr. It." She paused. "I swear."

Mr. Bit shook his head. The promises of a ten-year-old girl did not impress him much. And yet Flor detected a new gleam of respect in his eyes, for the mere fact that she came from a long line of math geniuses.

"I'd like to study your family's book a little more," Mr. Bit said now, "since I am an unwilling prisoner in Paris."

"Maybe you'll find some math formulas you didn't even know about."

"Not likely. I live so close to numbers, I know them all."

"Shall we go meet the future?" Dr. Pi put his arm around Flor and gave her a friendly squeeze, and kept his arm around her as they walked, as if trying to protect her from whatever was to come.

Chapter 14

OFF TO LA PALETTE FOR BREAKFAST

If a stranger had walked by La Palette that fine spring morning, they might have seen the odd foursome standing under a green and white awning, waiting for the café to open. They were truly a gypsy crew: a bald man with a beautiful lemon-colored shirt and striped tie. A skinny transparent gentleman in a white suit and white shoes, who seemed fascinated by a small book. Occasionally he'd jump up and cry out, "Brilliant! High five for the Bernoullis!" and then return to his reading. An attractive and thin lady in a black dress covered with a black cape accentuated with lace, wearing no shoes at all. And finally, a girl—also shoeless—dressed in beautiful pantaloons with a single teardrop earring on her left ear. She kept turning a blue and red hat in her hands and looking up and down the street.

"This charming street dates back to the thirteenth century," Dr. Pi said to Mrs. Plump. "And this particular bistro first opened in 1903, over a century ago. Ah, look, they are unrolling the awning, and starting to bring out chairs and tables. It shouldn't be long before we're settling down to croissants and tartines."

"I don't eat croissants and tartines," Mrs. Plump scoffed.

"Well, tea and toast, then."

"I have never sat down to breakfast without being fully dressed. I'm missing shoes. I can't eat with naked feet!"

"Would you like to try my shoes?"

"You're wearing slippers," she said. "That's one of your many strange habits. And your feet are big."

"My slippers shrink or grow to fit whatever feet they're on. Why don't you try them?"

Mrs. Plump looked doubtful, but she was desperate. "All right," she finally conceded.

Dr. Pi took his slippers off and knelt on the pavement. Mrs. Plump looked away and raised a reluctant foot. He slid the soft shoe on, gave it a pat, and watched it contract from a size ten to a size five.

Mrs. Plump looked down at her foot.

"Criminy!" she exclaimed, wiggling her toes. "Why, this slipper is the most comfortable thing I've worn in my entire life!"

"Shall I put the other one on?"

"Please do!"

Clad in slippers, Mrs. Plump looked ready to dance— or, at the very least, to eat breakfast.

"And what are *you* going to wear now?" Mr. Bit said, looking up for a moment from his book. "I suppose you're going to ask *me* to give you *my* shoes."

"My feet are perfectly happy to breathe in these silk socks," said Dr. Pi.

"Mine too," said Flor. "Look, the café is open. Let's get the best seats!"

Soon they found two small round tables under a large painting of the countryside. In fact, the bistro was filled with paintings, and the clocks had paintbrushes for hands.

"I should buy French café tables like this for my shop," said Mrs. Plump, looking around. "I'd like a gilt mirror like that one too. Look at those waiters in their crisp black-and-white uniforms. Why don't we have waiters like that in Brooklyn? Why, everything in Paris is absolutely to die for! When I get home I'm going on a decorating spree."

Her face was flushed with excitement. She'd never once traveled outside of New York. And now here she was, on a genuine vacation in Paris. It was surely one of the best mornings of her life.

The waiter inquired what they would like. Dr. Pi ordered sausages and mashed potatoes. Mr. Bit said a glass of water would be more than enough, and went back to his book. Flor wanted a strawberry tart and milk. Mrs. Plump hesitated.

"I'm a widely respected expert on tea," she said. "But the French don't drink much tea, do they?"

Coffee was more popular, the waiter admitted.

"Well then, I'll be daring and have an espresso," declared Mrs. Edna Plump.

The bistro was filling up with customers. Flor wasn't quite sure exactly how she would know her father.

"Is that a *tart*?" she heard Mrs. Plump saying. "It doesn't *look* like a tart. But it must be a tart. They have such an interesting way of doing things in Paris."

Flor looked down to see a wedge-shaped crust brushed with glistening jam and topped with a tumble of fresh strawberries. Thick cream had been ladled onto the side of her plate.

"Mmmm!" she said, diving in with her fork.

"As a baker, I can say that your dessert does give a new meaning to the word tart," said Dr. Pi with considerable interest. "The tart is a cousin of the pie. It's smaller and doesn't usually have a crust on top. These berries look like jewels. May I try a bite?"

"Sure. I think you could do this with your Sky-High Pies. Just put heaps of berries on top."

At that moment she heard a woman calling her dad's name. It rang out like a clear bell across the café.

"Jacques!" The words that followed were French, so Flor couldn't understand a single one. But she caught the tone. It was both affectionate and amused.

The woman who had called his name was slender, with almond-colored eyes and short blond hair. She wore a blue velvet jacket, white slacks, and a white lace camisole. She looked unbearably chic.

Holding her hand was a six-year-old girl with the same short blond hair and golden brown eyes, dressed in a blue dress and white Mary Jane shoes to match.

"Papa!" the girl called, in a voice as amused and musical as her mother's.

"He has a family?" Flor said haltingly. "He has a wife? And a daughter?"

She turned to Dr. Pi, her face darkening with anger.

"Why didn't you tell me?"

He looked uncomfortable. "I honestly didn't know how."

Flor's father had been lingering outside the café, talking to another couple.

Now he hurried in to catch up with his family. He had dark hair and sparkling brown eyes. He was so youthful and boyish he hardly seemed like anyone's father.

"I don't look like him," Flor said sadly. "I totally look like my mom."

She watched her father smile at the little girl and ruffle her hair—just like the fathers of Flor's friends at those summer barbecues.

"How can he do that right in front of me?"

"He doesn't know he's in front of you. But I, too, hate public displays of affection," Mrs. Plump agreed. "He seems to think his little girl is the cat's meow. The duck's quack, the bee's knees, the apple of his eye, and a hundred other clichés rolled into one."

The Bernoullis seated themselves a few tables away and ordered breakfast from a waiter who seemed to know them well. They waved to an older man at the bar. Two ladies passing by stopped to chat.

And now what? Did she just walk up and introduce herself? Perhaps this French wife of his wouldn't be happy to see her. Flor had a feeling that this woman didn't even know she existed. Her dad had probably never even mentioned that he had a daughter over in

America. He was talking and laughing and enjoying himself this sunny Paris morning, and it was obvious that not even one molecule in his brain was occupied with long-forgotten Flor.

Suddenly she was tired. It was too much trouble to lift her fork to spear a strawberry. She sank down into her chair, trying to make herself as small as possible.

"I want to go home," she said in a low voice. "Now."

"Having an attack of shyness?" Mr. Bit said suddenly, slapping the little book closed. "Wondering why, miss? I know exactly how that feels. Happens to me all the time. No idea what to say, no idea whether to go or stay. Well, how about if I do it for you?"

"You do what for me?"

"I'll make the introduction. He's nothing to me and everything to you. I have no feelings to hurt, while you have so many feelings someone could trip over them just walking past you. So it makes sense that I, who couldn't care less, should go over to your father. In fact, there's nobody but me to do it. I'm Mr. Bit, and in this case, I fit."

"Well . . ."

Mr. Bit stood. "That means yes. I know yes when I hear it."

She nodded to Mr. Bit gratefully.

He squared his shoulders, took a sip of water, and—famous little book in hand—went over to meet Jacques Bernoulli, the Parisian artist and father of a ten-year-old girl from Brooklyn, New York.

Chapter
15

AN EARRING FOR AIMÉE

Flor had suddenly become fascinated with her tart. All at once it seemed like a brilliant idea to cut the crispy crust into small rectangles and arrange them around the edge of her plate. Basically, crust-cutting was a great excuse to keep staring down and avoid any shocks or embarrassment.

And so the spying was left to Mrs. Plump and Dr. Pi, who were leaning as far as possible in the direction of the Bernoulli family's table. Mrs. Plump held her coffee cup to her lips, and forgot to take a sip. Dr. Pi's sausages and mashed potatoes lay, half-eaten, on his plate.

"Mr. Bit is waving your book at him," said Mrs. Plump.

"Your dad looks confused," said Dr. Pi.

"Mr. Bit is talking a mile a minute."

"Your dad's face has gone as white as Mr. Bit's suit."

"I think your father is telling Mr. Bit he doesn't believe him."

"His wife seems to be trying to calm them down. She must have invited Mr. Bit to join them—because that's what he just did. He just sat down."

"Your father is looking at the book. Mr. Bit is showing him your name in the last chapter, I think."

"The little girl is pointing at you."

"At me?" mumbled Flor, still absorbed in her crust-cutting mission.

"She just jumped off her chair and is running over to us," said Dr. Pi. "And her mother is running after her. Hmmm, she's an independent little one, isn't she? A bit like you."

Flor looked up. The girl was staring at her in a friendly, curious way.

"*Le monsieur a raison? T'es vraiment ma soeur?*"

Somehow Flor knew she was asking if they were truly sisters. She nodded slowly.

"*T'habites vraiment à New York, aux États-Unis?*"

Well, that one was easy enough to figure out—she must be asking if Flor really lived in New York.

She nodded again.

The girl jumped up and down in excitement. "*Maman!*" she cried. "*Maman, on peut y aller?*"

The woman took her daughter's hand. "Aimée," she said in a tone of gentle warning. She turned back to Flor. "I'm Jeanne. How did you find us here? And who are these people you're with?"

"We've known her since she was a baby," said Mrs. Plump. "I own a famous tea shop in her neighborhood. Dr. Pi is unfortunately just as famous for his fattening desserts as I am for my healthy teas. And Mr. Bit is . . . well, he's Mr. Bit. We were taking a quick trip to Paris. . . ."

"And I joined them," Flor added.

"Ah," said Jeanne to Dr. Pi and Mrs. Plump. "You look like a very nice couple. Have you been married for many years?" Mrs. Plump blushed at the thought of being linked romantically with Dr. Pi and started to correct her, but Flor interrupted.

"This is a café for artists, so we hoped my father might stop by. It looks like we hit the jackpot. We heard you call his name, and . . ."

Jeanne seemed to believe her. Just then Mr. Bit sauntered over, followed by Jacques, who indeed, had the book open to the chapter with Flor's name. He put it down on the table.

Mr. Bit sat. "I'm Mr. Bit, and I'm having fun, I admit."

He looked at Flor expectantly.

"Thanks," she mumbled.

"Although," he said, "it's time to go. Remember your promise, miss."

"Just one more minute," Flor begged.

"*Tiens, ma chérie,*" Jeanne said to her daughter, taking her hand. Flor thought Jeanne looked uncomfortable. She started to nudge her daughter toward the door.

Aimée shook her head stubbornly. Instead she tugged at her father's jacket sleeve. "*Papa, j'ai une grande soeur.*"

"You do have a big sister," Jacques agreed in English,

adding, "A ready-made big sister." He turned to his wife and said softly, "Please stay."

Aimée inched closer to Flor. *"Pourquoi tu n'es pas venue me voir plus tôt?"*

"I don't know what she's saying."

"She's asking," her father said slowly, "why you didn't come see her before now."

Flor wanted to dislike Aimée, oh, she wanted to dislike her so much, since Aimée possessed the one thing Flor desired. But Aimée was so friendly, the idea of a half sister from Paris was starting to sound maybe just a little bit all right.

Flor said to her father, "The Spiral. You sign every painting with it. Dr. Pi says it's part of my destiny. Is it part of yours?"

He nodded. "I sign everything I make with the Spiral. It brings me inspiration. Sometimes the Spirit of the Spiral comes into my dreams. Has it come into yours now too?"

"Not yet," admitted Flor.

"It will, no doubt it will."

Her dad's gaze grew distant, as if he was gazing on

something the rest of them could not see. "She's beautiful, the Spirit of the Spiral. She came to me first when I was a boy, and taught me to look to nature for all my art. Nature is the greatest artist of us all. That is why I like to work with stained glass, which lets natural sunlight and color change our world." He paused, and looked at her now as if waking from a dream. "Did you ever notice the spiral shape of the stained-glass skylight I built for your mother in Brooklyn?"

"I never did," Flor said, and she almost started to cry. "And now it's broken, Mr. Bit and Mr. It broke it, and I'll never have a chance to look at it again."

Her dad looked perplexed. He turned to Mr. Bit with raised eyebrows.

Mr. Bit explained, "My brother is all right, but not too good at flight. He had flown through too many wormholes and didn't adjust his speed when he came into Earth's atmosphere. We crashed through your skylight."

"Spiral, shmiral, skylight, shmylight," said Mrs. Plump. "What matters in life is virtue and moderation and how we treat each other. So I'd like to know why you think it was suitable to divorce your first wife and child and start a new family in Paris? And never call once? No cards? No visits? Ever?"

Flor looked down at her plate and began to arrange her rectangles of crust again. The truth was, she couldn't have been more grateful to the annoying Mrs. Plump for being so *very* annoying right now.

"We made a youthful mistake when we married," her father said slowly. "We were so young."

"Well, what happened?" asked Mrs. Plump, her tone still disapproving.

"It was a tale of two countries," he sighed. "She loved New York and I missed France. Then she got pregnant. She was so excited to have a baby. I asked her to move to France with me, but she felt she could never adapt to French life. She said she would raise Flor on her own. I didn't know if it was wise to be a part-time father from France. It seemed so awkward. We decided this way was best."

Everybody was silent.

"Well," said Mrs. Plump. "Well, well, well."

"I did not know you ever thought of me," Jacques said unhappily.

"Yes," Flor said in a low voice. "I thought of you." Then she looked right into his dark brown eyes. "You don't have to . . . raise me. I'm mostly raised anyway. But you could visit me."

"But of course," he said.

"Of course!" echoed Jeanne.

"And I'd be happy to make you a new stained-glass skylight, with spirals all across it," he offered.

"You would?"

"But of course," he said again.

"But course!" imitated Aimée.

"I'm Mr. Bit, and I'm in a snit," came a warning voice. "It's getting late!"

Flor couldn't help laughing. Mr. Bit's style was all his own. "Okay, we have to go," she said.

"We're going to meet Mr. It, who is Mr. Bit's twin brother," Dr. Pi explained. "He's not feeling well."

Flor turned to Aimée. "Here," she said, unclipping her earring and holding it out. "This is for you."

Aimée grinned and reached for the earring. She turned it over carefully in her hands and then gave Flor a quick, shy hug.

"You will *love* my outfits," Flor said, suddenly inspired. "When I outgrow them, I'll save them for you."

She was certain Aimée understood her. They stared deep into each other's eyes and smiled. The bond was sealed.

Everyone said their good-byes, with kisses on both cheeks for all. Then Flor and her friends hurried out the door.

Chapter

16

LET'S ALL HAVE A GOOD CRY

The future seems to have adapted to your wishes. That went amazingly well," said Dr. Pi as they each climbed into the magic hat, which immediately stretched to accommodate them.

"You think so?" said Flor.

"I do. I feared the worst."

"Well, for once, Dr. Pi, you couldn't be more wrong!" And she burst into tears.

"She's crying," said Mr. Bit nervously. "I've never shed a tear. I don't know how. I never fear."

Dr. Pi looked stunned.

"It's awful!" Flor sobbed.

She hung her head and bawled.

"We're supposed to be flying. But she's crying, she's crying," Mr. Bit repeated anxiously.

"What is it?" asked Dr. Pi. "He could have ignored you, or his wife could have been jealous. They said they'd come visit. And your sister is adorable."

"It's obvious what's wrong," announced Mrs. Plump. "Can't you two insensitive males see?"

Dr. Pi seemed totally flummoxed. "Flor?"

Mrs. Plump coughed loudly. "'What happens to a dream deferred? Does it dry up, like a raisin in the sun?' Flor had a dream."

Flor nodded, sniffling and snuffling. "That's wight, I had a dweam," she said through her sniffling and snuffling.

"She had her future all worked out. Her dashing French dad was going to meet her in one of her to-die-for outfits, and marvel over his gem of a daughter. They'd have a long, intimate talk to make up for lost time. He'd invite her to come live with him in France, or decide to move back to America just to be near her. He'd keep shaking his head and saying to himself—"

"'How did I ever leave her in Brooklyn?'" burst out Flor. "But he doesn't feel that way at all. He has his own wife and daughter."

And she burst into a fresh round of weeping.

"He can't love you the first hour," said Dr. Pi. "He will come to love you over time, I'm sure."

"One plus two equals three," said Mr. Bit. "One plus two equals three. Oh my oh my oh me oh me. One plus two equals three."

"Stop counting," Mrs. Plump snapped. "What's wrong with you?"

"I can't help it. She's making me nervous. She's crying so much our hat will flood with tears and we'll drown."

"I know just how you feel, Flor," Mrs. Plump said quietly.

"You can't possibly."

"Oh yes I can."

Flor looked up, rubbing her nose with the back of her hand. "How can you?"

"It happened to me."

"What happened to you?"

"My father left my mother, although not until I was twelve years old. He fell in love with somebody else and that was that. He did send money and Christmas presents, but they didn't make it better. That's why I've always felt . . . a special affection for you. I saw you around the neighborhood with your mom, and no father."

"And so what did you do?" asked Flor.

"We cried and we ate sweets," said Mrs. Plump simply.

"They ate?" echoed Mr. Bit, astounded. "What does eating have to do with a missing father?"

Mr. Bit looked very peeved. He had lived his whole life not understanding people's peculiar ways. And here it was again—people doing things that made no sense at all.

"People eat to stay alive," he said. "Why do they eat when they're sad? I'm Mr. Bit, and I don't get it!"

"It's like your rhymes, Mr. Bit," Mrs. Plump explained. "You rhyme for fun, you rhyme to calm yourself down.

Well, for some of us, a delicious sweet or a piece of pie is the same."

"It's like my rhymes?" He thought for a minute. "For the first time, I understand. I feel so odd, being more numbers than man. My parents liked my brother better. I was strange because they could see right through me to the other side. They forced me to eat, but I spit it out. But my brother, Mr. It . . ." He trailed off, then finally concluded, "He understands me without trying. He doesn't ask why I'm the way I am. Mr. It loves Mr. Bit just as he is . . . skinny, tall, numbers, rhymes, snits and all."

"And it's clear Mr. Bit loves Mr. It right back," said Dr. Pi. "Let me add my two cents—or two bits, in honor of you, Mr. Bit—to our conversation."

"You're always jolly, Dr. Pi," said Flor. "I know you don't have a single sorrow."

"Oh, but I do," he said gently. "I come from a line of wizards. The Bernoullis were, once upon a time, distant cousins of ours. Flor, in my family we live for thousands of centuries. When I was given the task of guarding the Spiral and tending to the fire, I was told that I must go far away. There was someone out there who wanted to steal the fire and destroy the Spiral. Or at the very least take it for himself and control it and rule it."

"That isn't me," said Mr. Bit. "I don't want to destroy a thing."

"I know that now," said Dr. Pi. "The enemy of the Spiral is still out there searching for me. And so, I had to leave my family. I came to this little corner of planet Earth and made a new life. I had to pretend to be only a baker of pies. Every Sunday I beam a warm hello to my brothers and sisters and they beam me back, but I don't get to visit them. And I faced the prospect of living through thousands of years of this loneliness. Until today, I had not one friend here who really knew me—for who I am."

They were all silent, contemplating the ways they were different on the outside and yet the same on the inside.

"Now I have three real friends," said Dr. Pi. "It's a new day, indeed. Shall we be on our way?"

And with that the magic hat rose, hovered in midair, and began to spin its way home.

Chapter
17

FLOR MEETS THE MILKY WAY

Dr. Pi was a much better navigator of magic hats than Flor. They spun smoothly, and the hat was just the right size for everybody to fit without feeling cramped. Even Mr. Bit had plenty of room for his skinny legs and sharp elbows, which stuck out as he went back to reading the history of the Bernoullis.

Mrs. Plump had gotten sleepy. Flor saw her eyes flutter shut and her head nod forward, then bob to the side, then nod forward, until it came to rest on Dr. Pi's shoulder, where it stayed.

"What I wouldn't give for a camera now!" said Flor. "She'd be mortified!"

Mrs. Plump snored softly, blissfully unaware.

"Look at this," Mr. Bit said suddenly. "Your chapter has a beginning now!"

"It does?"

He handed the book to her.

"It does!" She read out loud, "'The Spiral so beloved by Jakob Bernoulli inspired many later generations of Bernoullis. In the early twenty-first century, Jacques Bernoulli's firstborn child, the American girl Flor Bernoulli, had her first true encounter with the Spiral at the Lighthouse of the Whales on the Île de Ré off the coast of France. She was ten years old at the time. The Special Spiraling Hat, given to Dr. Pi by his father, spun her to a spiral staircase composed of two hundred fifty-seven steps. There Flor stood and looked upon a spiral of immense proportions. The Special Spiraling Hat then took her to meet her father, Jacques, and her half sister, Aimée, at a café in Paris. On her way back to Brooklyn, accompanied by her companions Dr. Pi,

Mrs. Plump, and Mr. Bit, Flor had a close encounter with the Spiral itself. This was to change her life forever.'"

Flor looked up. "A close encounter. I haven't had any close encounter."

"Does it end there?" asked Dr. Pi.

She looked down. "The next sentence is only half a sentence."

"Let me see," said Mr. Bit, snatching the book back. "It says, 'After she opened the zipper of the Special Spiraling Hat's pocket and stepped onto the unfolding stairs . . .'"

He looked up. "Well, unzip the pocket, and step onto the stairs! Don't you want to know what happens?"

Flor looked at Dr. Pi. "How has something appeared in the book before I actually did it?"

"The book has gotten a little bit ahead of you, that's all."

"What if I decide *not* to open the zipper? Will the sentence disappear?"

Dr. Pi thought for a moment. "You can do that. But

when our true destiny steps up to meet us, it's difficult to run away."

"You and your wise sayings," she grumbled. "I guess I might as well. . . ."

Flor pulled the zipper open. As she did so, the little staircase popped out of the pocket and began to expand like an accordion.

She stepped onto the top stair.

The Special Spiraling Hat paused in midair. Its top step surged upward as hundreds of steps opened and unfolded below. Then the entire staircase swiveled, and Flor found herself standing outside the hat in a pure blue sky, high as could be.

Now the staircase was expanding so fast, with so many steps flying out under her, that she dropped to her knees and grabbed the edges of the step in order to stop herself from flying off into space like a speck of dust. A fierce wind howled, and her hair blew and snapped against her face. She looked back and saw her three companions, their heads bobbing up at the rim of the hat, their faces astonished. But now she was so far away they looked like three little buttons. And a moment later she was even farther away than that. The hat had disappeared, with her friends inside it.

She was somewhere in outer space, absolutely alone in bitter cold and headed for a collision with a swirling mass of stars ahead.

Chapter
18

INSIDE THE SPIRIT OF THE SPIRAL

Don't be afraid," she heard a voice inside her head. "You're right where you belong."

"Where is that?" She seemed to be skidding pell-mell through billions of stars that were hurtling past her like a blizzard. She flew right through them and out again to the other side, where it was warm as a spring day.

A skirt billowed out before her. Flor's eyes followed the skirt round and round and up and up. It flowed into a sheer blouse with long ribbony sleeves, and up to a face as white as the moon.

But even more remarkable were the numbers. Numbers seemed to whirl around the woman like hula hoops. They seemed to be chasing each other, zeros flinging themselves at ones, twos, and threes. The numbers seemed full of joy. She could almost feel their delight. And then, all at once, every number paused, and out of them began to unfurl the most remarkable spiral.

Flor was so astounded she forgot to be afraid.

"If I could add a skirt like that to my outfits," she said to the woman, "I'd be the talk of my entire school. Who are you?"

"Who else but the Spirit of the Spiral?"

"My father said you'd come."

"I'm going to take you on a journey."

"Where to?"

"To show you my many homes." The woman held out her hand. "You just journeyed through the spiral galaxy that is the Milky Way. There are a hundred billion stars in the Milky Way. Your galaxy, and many others, look like they have long curving arms. Those arms are actually made of millions of young, brightly burning stars. Look back and you'll see the whole galaxy from a distance."

She looked back. A chasm of stars, like brilliant snow, arced across an infinite night sky. "Unbelievable."

"Now, would you like to go inside an ear?"

"Can I get back out? I wouldn't like to be stuck inside an ear forever."

The woman laughed. "Come on," she said, and Flor took her hand again. "The next time somebody whispers in your ear, think cochlea."

"Ummm . . . think what?"

"Cochlea. It comes from the Greek word for snail. It's the name for a tiny, spiral-shaped tube like a snail's shell, deep inside your ear. Its spiral shape allows whispers and soft, low sounds to echo loudly so that you can hear them better. Come on in."

Suddenly she was swimming through a warm thick fluid inside a curving chamber. She swam along toward the center. She heard a faraway whisper, almost like wind, but could not decipher the words. But slowly it grew louder, and the fluid formed waves, carrying the voice, which was very clearly upset:

"I did not ever put my head on *your* shoulder to sleep! I have better manners than that!"

The voice was Mrs. Plump's.

"Whose ear am I inside?" Flor asked the Spirit.

"Dr. Pi's ear. I thought he would enjoy the joke when you see him again."

"So Mrs. Plump is denying she fell asleep on Dr. Pi's shoulder?"

"Yes—exactly. Do you want to stay here for a while, or visit another home of mine?"

"It's pretty weird being inside Dr. Pi's ear," Flor admitted. "Can we go somewhere else—whoa! Where are we now?"

"We're inside a hawk's eye."

"Inside a hawk's eye? Awesome!" She almost forgot to ask, "Why am I inside a hawk's eye, anyway?"

"Because the hawk flies in a spiral shape, round and round and down and down, to catch its prey. Watch— you can see just what the hawk is seeing."

"Why does it fly in a spiral instead of a straight line?"

"A hawk dives at high speed, and it doesn't want to turn its head to keep its eye on its prey. So instead it keeps its head straight and flies in a spiral."

And it went on and on like that. She landed in a spiderweb, glistening and sticky, because a spider spins its web in a spiral. She went into the center of a sunflower, where its seeds grew clockwise in two directions and made a spiral, and then she went to the mountains of Africa, where a plant called spiral aloe grew, its spiky leaves going round and round and up and up. They even visited a herd of rams, and Flor could see at once that their thick horns curved round in a spiral shape.

To think it all could be described by one math equation.

"So math . . . math gives the universe its building blocks? Numbers are kind of like the bricks you use to build a house? Or like the ingredients you use to bake a pie?"

"Yes, kind of." She heard the Spirit chuckling.

Flor turned to her.

"And where is the fire?" she asked. "The fire that some-how breathes life into everything?"

"We aren't speaking of fire in a fireplace or candle."

"Well, what kind of fire is it?"

"Fire is another word for the energy that flows through the entire universe, and brings everything to life."

Flor sort of got it, but it sounded so cosmic. "That's so vague, though."

"It does sound a bit vague," the Spirit agreed. "Because it's impossible to describe in words. Just look around you. Our universe is a sea of energy. When Mr. Bit asked you what breathes fire into the equations, he was really asking you where the energy comes from that makes this all so alive. How does the seashell know to follow the same math that the sunflower follows? Will we ever really understand?"

Flor thought about that for a while. "I guess not."

"So, we must just live it."

"Can you take me into the fire so I can feel it?"

The Spirit hesitated.

"I would understand it then," said Flor. "Even if I had no words for it."

"Yes, but you are very young, even if you have a big destiny. I am not sure you are skilled enough to withstand the heart of the fire."

Flor sighed.

"You will go into the heart of the fire, though," the Spirit promised her. "Someday soon, you will."

"I think this is all a little too much for me. I kind of want my own, boring life back, you know? I really want to go home and be in my own bed, and do my homework and pet Libenits the cat until he purrs, and see my mom. Isn't my mom worried about me? She must be out of her mind with worry. I can't save Mr. It and ruin all these spirals. And I don't want to be with Mr. Bit when his brother just dies on him. He's going to be heartbroken. He's a nice guy when you get past those weird habits of his. It's all just impossible. Can't you take me home?"

"Is that really what you want?"

Flor thought about it.

"I can't abandon them. But I have no clue what to do!"

"That's the exciting part. Your chapter is yours to write. It's up to you now."

"Oh great," Flor sighed, "just what I wanted to hear."

"Are you ready?" asked the Spirit.

Flor nodded, even though she wasn't.

Suddenly she found herself hurtling pell-mell through the blizzard of stars again and speeding like a missile right through the atmosphere of Mother Earth, over America, down along the East Coast, zooming in like a movie camera to the study on the top floor of the Sky-High Pie Shop in Brooklyn.

And there she landed.

Chapter
19

MR. BIT MAKES A BAD DECISION

Mr. It was still alive, but just barely. Stretched out in Dr. Pi's soft, scuffed leather recliner, his eyes were shut and his breathing shallow. Flor wasn't surprised to see her three friends waiting for her. Dr. Pi's Special Spiraling Hat was back on his head where it belonged. A still messy Mrs. Plump had somehow obtained a cup of tea, which she now gratefully sipped, sighing with pleasure. Mr. Bit was kneeling at his brother's side.

Mr. It's eyes fluttered open, and then slowly drooped shut again. Mr. Bit looked at Flor, and she could almost hear his silent reproach: *You found your father, now I lose my brother?*

"His time is nearly up," said Mr. Bit. "My math was wrong. The fire has disappeared much faster than I thought."

Mr. It groaned. "Your math was right. I just didn't rest, like I promised."

"Well, what did you do?" asked Flor.

"Snooped on Dr. Pi's computer," he whispered. "I know I shouldn't have . . . used the last of my energy to crack his password . . . thought I could save myself. . . . He keeps a diary. . . ."

"You keep a diary!" exclaimed Mrs. Plump. "Why would you do a thing like that?"

"Am I the only one who writes down their thoughts when alone at night?" asked Dr. Pi.

She looked away, embarrassed.

"So what did you discover?" asked Flor.

"He took a vow . . . must protect the fire with his life . . ." Mr. It closed his eyes. Then he summoned up enough energy to add, "I worry . . . about Mr. Bit . . . all alone . . . when I'm gone . . ."

"He can live with me," Dr. Pi offered.

"Let him come live with *me*," said Flor.

"He can even live with me, if it comes to that," offered Mrs. Plump. "His white contrasts well with my black."

"Three invitations," said Mr. Bit. "That's three more than I've ever had. I'm not so bad?"

"Not bad at all," said Flor. "But we can't give up on your brother." Suddenly she had an idea. "Let me see my book. Does my chapter say anything new? Where do the sentences stop now?"

He handed her the book. She quickly thumbed to the end.

"'Upon her return to Brooklyn,'" Flor read out loud, "'the Bernoulli girl found Mr. It only minutes from death, the last of his fire ebbing away. She turned to Dr. Pi,'" and now Flor turned to Dr. Pi and went on reading: "'And she said, "Where did you hide the fire? You stuck it in another dimension, but where is that dimension? Because we've got to go there now and get fire for Mr. It."'"

The rest of the sentence was faint, barely visible, like

watermarks. She squinted and tried her best to read. "'The magic key . . . was . . . the only answer.'"

As she read the words out loud, the sentence darkened, until the type was clear and black on the page.

"Spooky. Totally spooky," said Flor. "Dr. Pi, we must go get the fire right this second."

"I must go alone," he said.

"I'm going with you!"

He put his hand up gently. "It's in another dimension that is rolled up very tiny, like a little ball of string, and if you tried to make yourself that tiny, you wouldn't survive. I'm a wizard and can do such things. But when I come back—I can do nothing. It's all up to you, then. I can't break my vow. I can't even tell you what to do."

"The key," said Flor. "Can you give me the key?"

He looked at his watch and took his hat off, unzipped the secret compartment, handed her the key, and climbed into the hat. "I'll be back in five minutes."

And with that, he flew off.

Flor held the key tightly in her fist, and went over to Mr. It and felt his forehead. It was cold as marble. Even his breath was chilled, as if it had been cooled on ice.

Mrs. Plump came forward to touch Mr. It. "He's a refrigerator!" she gasped. "Here, Mr. It, you poor fellow, at least this blanket should help."

"How much time does he have left?"

"He's down to his last ember. He's hardly with us now," Mr. Bit said. "See how peaceful he looks? He feels no pain."

Flor sat down. This couldn't really be happening.

All I cared about was going to meet my dad and how he was going to adore me, she thought. *Mr. Bit put up with me the whole trip. He let me fly on his back. He even went and introduced himself to my dad when I was too scared. I mean, I could have visited my dad anytime if I really wanted. I've never once asked my mom to call him for me. I was scared to hurt her feelings, 'cause I think she still loves my dad after all these years. Now Mr. Bit is about to lose the only person who ever loved him. And even if Dr. Pi gets back in time, how are we going to breathe fire into Mr. It like they do on Planet Dog?*

She opened her hand and stared down at the key. Somehow this key held the answer.

"'*Eadem mutata resurgo semperdem,*'" she said out loud, reading the now familiar inscription on the key. "I shall arise again the same, though changed. Always."

Mr. Bit looked at her.

"I really screwed up, didn't I?" she said.

Mr. Bit walked over to the windows and pulled the curtain, looking out onto the street with its rows of brownstones and pleasant stoops decorated with flowerpots. He watched two children on their bikes, laughing.

"It's a strange, strange place, no matter where I go. I'm a strange, strange man no matter what I know. I can't erase who I am. What's done is done. There's only one way out," he said at last.

Flor looked at him closely. "What way is that?"

"Mr. It is like the rest of you. I'm not. I don't want to go on without him. No matter whose house I live in. I'm Mr. Bit, I just don't fit. So, that's it."

Mrs. Plump slammed down her teacup. She said in her most scolding voice, "What do you mean, that's it? Don't you dare do what I think you are thinking of doing. That's simply not allowed." She added primly, "The first rule of a virtuous life is to respect all life—that includes your own! That is the Way of Tea and Toast."

Mr. Bit shook his head and repeated firmly, "I'm Mr. Bit, I just don't fit."

He went over to his brother and blew as hard as he could. He blew and he blew, and as he blew, Flor saw color flush Mr. It's face. His eyes flew open, and he began to move his fingers and stretch.

"I feel better! It's positively warm in here! Open a window already," he exclaimed—and then, as his brother blew out his last breath, Mr. It shouted, "Mr. Bit, what have you done! You promised not to! Don't do that for me!"

For even as Mr. It came back to life, and even as Mr. Bit blew his last puff of fire into his brother to save him, he began to turn back to numbers. Flor watched in horror as Mr. Bit broke apart into pieces. And then each piece turned into numbers. He was all threes and fours and sevens, all twos and sixes and eights. Numbers shimmered in rows and columns in midair for an incredible forever-moment, thousands and thousands of shining numbers, before they fell all at once in a heap to the floor.

The ice-cream suit crumpled on top of them, with two white shoes sticking out.

Mr. Bit was no more.

Chapter

20

THE CIRCLE DANCE

I'm back," said a breathless Dr. Pi, as he climbed out of the magic hat and put it on his head. "I've got the fire."

"You're too late," said Mrs. Plump. "Mr. Bit is dead!"

"Mr. *Bit*? Do you mean Mr. *It*?"

"My brother sacrificed himself to save me, sir," said Mr. It. "And there are his remains, upon the floor. All that's left of him are some numbers."

Mr. It sat down and began to gather the numbers up in his hands. Flor and Mrs. Plump knelt down next to him, scooping up numbers and putting them on the table.

"I miss him already," said Flor. "His funny rhymes. 'I'm Mr. Bit, I'm in a snit.'"

The numbers in her hands danced a little as she said that. Perplexed, she repeated herself. "'I'm Mr. Bit, I'm in a snit.'"

No doubt about it, the numbers moved. They kind of flexed and fell against one another. It was almost like they were laughing.

"Dr. Pi!" she said. "I think he's still here, sort of . . . in a very odd way that I don't understand. . . . Mr. It, do you think we still have a chance to bring him back?"

"I don't know," said Mr. It. "I've never seen someone come back from the dead. We don't have that kind of magic on my planet."

"It's possible," said Dr. Pi. "Things change form, but they never really die. Clouds form from water droplets, rain falls into the lake, winter comes and the lake turns to ice, summer comes and the lake turns to water. All things change form, and sometimes we call that death, but . . ."

"Well, if that's true, then please, Dr. Pi, show me the fire. Maybe we can still fix Mr. Bit."

"The fire is right here," he said.

"Well, I don't see it!" Flor complained, very irritated.

"Dear, dear Flor," said Dr. Pi, "I can't tell you more. I *cannot* break my vow." He looked very unhappy. "I promise you, it's here," he added.

"Well, I never . . ." Flor turned to Mrs. Plump. "Make him tell me, please! Be your most annoying self!"

Mrs. Plump picked up her teacup again. "I'm thinking, I'm thinking," she said.

"Me too," said Flor. A key, a key, what is a key for? Well, obviously a key opens a lock. So this key must open a lock she hadn't yet found, to a container for the fire. Where was that locked container, what did it look like, and how would she find it?

She turned to Dr. Pi. "How much time do I have until Mr. Bit's numbers lose their last bit of life?"

He smiled. "Not a lot of time, but more than enough for a Bernoulli."

"Mr. It, Mrs. Plump, I need your help," said Flor. "I

only used the magic key once, to open the doors to Dr. Pi's shop. But it clearly opens something else, and inside that something else is the fire. And so we've got to find it, now! We've got to search every nook and cranny of this entire house and look for anything locked. Mrs. Plump, you start downstairs in the front of the shop. Mr. It, can you take the second floor? I'll search all the rooms here on the third floor. Meet me back here in fifteen minutes.

"And Dr. Pi, well . . . it's obvious you can't help without breaking some law of the universe or whatever." She shook her head. "The one thing you could do for me is walk over to my place and tell my mom I'm okay. Could you do that?"

He smiled, beamed at her actually, as if he couldn't be more proud. He looked kind of like those dads at summer barbecues as they gazed at their lovely daughters.

"Sure," he said, "I'll go round to your mom right away. And I'll see you there not long after, I expect."

The hunt was on. Mrs. Plump hurried down to the first floor, and Mr. It to the second. Flor began to search

Dr. Pi's study. In no time at all they had searched all the locks:

The old cash register. No fire in there.

A tin box of recipes on index cards—but the lock was broken, and nothing special was inside.

Every single door had a lock, and although the magic key fit each one, no room revealed any hidden fire.

They found a padlock secured to Dr. Pi's old bicycle.

An old silver chain with thick links had a tiny lock on it, with a keyhole way too small for the magic key.

There were locks on Dr. Pi's luggage in his closet, all useless.

"Nothing," said Flor. She sat down in Dr. Pi's recliner, near the heap of numbers. "'I'm Mr. Bit, I'm in a snit,'" she said, testing. The numbers on the table glowed briefly.

"He still seems to be here with us," said Mr. It, patting the numbers.

"We left his suit on the floor," Mrs. Plump said with a frown, and picked it up and shook it out. She folded it neatly. "Such a fine suit, pure linen."

Flor closed her eyes. Images buzzed into her mind:

swirling pies and ears, spinning galaxies and hats, spider-webs and hawks in flight.

What was the answer?

Where was the lock?

The key held the answer, but to what?

She turned the key in her hands. Above the two copper teeth was a small wheel, with metal leaves going round in a spiral. On top was a metal crown with a fleur-de-lis and a small knob. Flor turned the knob, and the top came off. Out fell a small scroll.

She unrolled it and read the tiny print out loud: "'To light the fire, all persons present must hold hands and form a circle, each facing outward. They must turn to the east, north, west, and south, repeating *"Eadem mutata resurgo semperdem"* in each direction, which will call upon the four winds. The winds will blow until the fire appears in the center of the circle.'"

Flor looked at her two companions.

"We have no time to lose," said Mrs. Plump. "We may look like fools, and nothing may happen, but we must try it."

And so they joined hands, each facing outward, repeating the magic words that were inscribed on Jakob Bernoulli's gravestone so long ago. They turned to the east, north, west, and south, again and again, and soon they found themselves dancing in a circle, laughing and singing out the words, *"Eadem mutata resurgo semperdem!"* A mysterious joy, a kind of euphoria, seemed to flow like an electric current from their hearts through their hands and back to their hearts. The room was warm but not hot, bright but not blinding. A pleasant breeze wafted the curtains. Flor and Mr. It and Mrs. Plump danced like they had never danced in all their lives. They danced as one. Round and round, faster and faster, dancing and singing, *"Eadem mutata resurgo semperdem. Eadem mutata resurgo semperdem. Eadem mutata resurgo semperdem."*

And then it appeared, out of nowhere. A flicker in the center of the circle. The flicker turned to flame. The flame became a fire. The fire rose up in long tongues of orange with tips of blue. It rose to the ceiling and engulfed Flor, Mrs. Plump, and Mr. It, and filled them to the very brim, inside them, around them, everywhere.

Flor let go of the others' hands. She was so full of the fire's strange power, its wonderful heat, that she spun around in pure joy. She knew what she had to do.

Chapter
21

MR. BIT IS A NEW MAN

Spinning like a top, Flor lifted her hands and blew onto the numbers that were once Mr. Bit. Orange and blue flame flowed out of her. The ones and twos and threes began to lift into the air. She spun around and blew and blew. The fours and fives went aloft. All the sixes and sevens and eights and nines followed. The numbers rose and formed a curtain from the ceiling to the floor. She blew and blew, and they began to join together and turn into parts. An ear, an eye, a chin. A finger, a mouth, a hip. They clicked into place. She kept blowing. Soon a very skinny, pale, see-through

Mr. Bit appeared. As he did, his white suit jumped off the table and onto his body.

"What the—?" he said. "Wasn't I dead?"

But Flor did not stop blowing. She spun around and blew more fire into Mr. Bit. And as she did so, he began to fill in. She blew until she couldn't see through him anymore. She blew until the buttons of his suit popped, and his white shirt turned bright blue. A bow tie appeared at his neck, and a stopwatch with a chain dangled from his pants pocket. She blew until his blond hair grew into thick waves around his face, and his lips turned warm with color, and his eyes sparkled. She went on blowing until, just as suddenly as it had arrived, the fire seemed to ebb away.

Mr. Bit now looked very rugged and handsome. He tugged at his sleeves. He straightened his bow tie. He coughed. He did a few knee bends and ran his fingers through his hair. He took out his new stopwatch, stared at it, shook his head, then put it back in his pocket. And finally he took a few unsteady steps, on stiff legs, like a toddler when he first learns to walk.

"This is too weird. I disappeared. I was nothing but

numbers. I'm not myself. I'm not recognizable at all! I'm somebody else! This isn't my shirt, this isn't my suit, and I've gotten too cute! Am I still Mr. Bit? Where is my snit? I don't get it."

Flor grinned. "You're real, at last. You're complete. You're all Mr. Bit."

"The new Mr. Bit!" agreed Mrs. Plump. "And much more fashionable. A dandy, almost!"

"I liked the old Mr. Bit," he fretted.

"Give the new you a chance," said Mr. It, admiring his brother. "You saved me and we're still together. Isn't that what counts?"

"And you still talk in ridiculous rhymes," Mrs. Plump noted, "so surely you're the same man deep down."

"Different but the same." Mr. Bit sighed. "I guess I could get used to this."

Then he turned to the others.

"I'm hungry," he said. "I want food." He paused. "I can't believe I said that."

"I have fabulous toast!" crowed Mrs. Plump. "Let's go to my place."

"Ugh," Flor groaned.

"I'll eat anything, as long as I can eat it now," said Mr. Bit. "Toast sounds fine."

They went downstairs. Flor snatched her platform shoes and made sure to lock the doors behind her with the magic key. Then they slipped into Mrs. Plump's Tea and Toast shop, where they sat at the small tables. Mrs. Plump opened a tin of rye crisps.

"It's a little like Paris, isn't it?" she said hopefully.

Flor shook her head. "Not at all."

"You'll help me redecorate?"

"Sure."

"My Dog!" said Mr. Bit. "My Dog!"

"What?" they said in unison.

He was chewing his rye toast.

"This is delicious!"

Flor giggled.

"This is the first food I ever ate that I didn't spit out," he admitted. "Is all food this good?"

"You're actually eating about the worst-tasting, flavorless food there is. Wait until you try fruit pie," Flor said, setting the magic key down on the table and lacing up her platform shoes. "My shoes are not black," she said to Mrs. Plump, "but you must admit they're fabulous, and they make the outfit."

"I must admit it," she said agreeably. "There is occasionally a purpose for silver shoes. And you seem to have found that occasion. And please, call me Edna."

"Dadgum, dadgum, dadgum, this rye toast sure is madgum."

"Madgum?" said Flor.

"It rhymes," said Mr. Bit. "What I mean is, this toast is great."

Flor looked at her watch. "I'd better be getting home. Hopefully Dr. Pi has explained things to my mom, but I have a feeling I'm in major trouble anyway. Would you guys come with me? I could use the support."

"Of course!" they said in unison, and were soon on their way.

Chapter
22

CREAKY CHICKEN DELIGHT

When Flor walked into her living room, her mother was seated with Dr. Pi on the couch, deep in conversation. But as soon as she saw Flor, she said loudly, "You're grounded."

"Well, I expected that."

"I was worried sick about you and had the police searching the entire neighborhood."

Flor grimaced.

"It was the worst night of my entire life," her mother went on. "I thought you might be an Amber Alert. A missing child. However, Dr. Pi has explained everything to me, and I mean everything. I have to say, if I wasn't so upset with you I would be proud of you, and in fact, I am."

"Really?"

"Don't you think I want my daughter to be a brave and generous heroine? Of course I do. However, the next time you decide to run off to save the world *and* meet your father, tell me first. At least I'll know where you are."

"Okay, Mom. I'm really sorry."

"And truthfully, it is the most amazing story I've ever heard, and if I hadn't known Dr. Pi for all these years, I'd think he was crazy. But after Dr. Pi told me the story, I tracked your dad down and called him for the first time in years and . . . it's true . . . you were there! Unbelievable!"

Her mom let out a long breath and shook her head. Then she said softly, "I need to apologize to *you* for something."

"What's that?"

"I thought you and I were enough, just us two together. I didn't purposely keep your father from you, I just thought it was simpler for all of us." She sighed. "I was so wrong."

"It's all right, Mom. We can talk about it later when I'm . . . grounded."

"Grounded," Mr. Bit echoed amiably. "That's really unfounded. She saved my life. Brought me back from numbers!" He stretched and tugged on his sleeves. "Hey, pie man, tell Flor's mother, am I not a new man?"

"Yes, indeed, you're a new man."

"He weighs twice as much as me now!" said Mr. It.

"And he's still less than half of me," Dr. Pi said with a smile.

"As you may have noticed, I'm missing my snit. It's totally gone. No snit. All I can say is, I'm Mr. Bit and wow, I fit."

"How did you save his life, Flor?" her mom asked.

"Let's give credit where credit is due," said Edna Plump. "We all did it together. We were a marvelous team, Mr. It, little Flor, and, of course, myself."

"What exactly did you do?"

"We blew fire into the numbers, Mom."

Her mom looked completely confused.

"But it wasn't like fire in a fireplace. It was more like . . . energy."

"I hate to interrupt," said Mr. Bit, "but I'm starved. I'm ravenous. I have to eat. I need some meat. I'm really hungry. My stomach is growling. I never ate before in my entire life, so I need to make up for lost time. Do you have anything edible?"

"I have leftover Chinese," she said. "Flor disappeared before she could eat her dinner."

"I ordered Creaky Chicken with hot sauce," said Flor. "If you liked those awful rye crisps, you'll think you died and went to heaven over Creaky Chicken."

"Why is it creaky?" asked Mr. Bit innocently. "Is it very old? Does it have bones?"

"No, silly, it's stir-fried until it's so crisp it practically creaks. Should we warm it up or do you prefer it cold?"

"I want it *now*," he said. "Temperature is irrelevant! Food of any kind, please!"

"Done," said Flor, and scurried into the kitchen, bringing back a plate of Creaky Chicken and rice.

Mr. Bit scooped up a handful of chicken and shoved it into his mouth and promptly seemed to lose his mind and begin gurgling like a baby.

"Rummmm . . . yummmmm . . . scrammmmm . . . onggggg . . . ockkkkk!"

This went on for a few minutes. Suddenly his face fell.

"My plate is empty. I've finished all my food. Now what do I do?"

"Let me get you some cherry cola," said Flor.

"Cherry cola?" he replied doubtfully.

"Trust me," Flor reassured him. "I was right about Creaky Chicken, wasn't I?"

"I'd like some cherry cola too," said Mr. It.

"Me too," said Dr. Pi.

"I wouldn't mind some myself," said Flor's mom. "I'll go get a six-pack for all of us."

And that was that. Not long after they were all seated on the floor, one big happy family, drinking cherry cola and listening to Mr. Bit rave about Creaky Chicken Delight.

Epilogue

DR. PI AND MRS. PLUMP'S SKY-HIGH PIE, TOAST, AND TEA SHOP

What a perfect June afternoon. It was almost three o'clock and it was Wednesday. There was no finer hour of the afternoon than three o'clock, especially on a Wednesday. For that was when the tart scent of fruit pie floated through the windows of Flor's school and did a dance right under her nose. That was the hour that Dr. Pi and Mrs. Plump opened their Sky-High Pie, Toast, and Tea Shop.

Flor was sitting in math class, watching Mr. Fineman draw spirals on the shiny white board.

"Does anybody know how to make a spiral out of a rectangle?" he asked.

Flor's hand shot up.

"Flor?" He seemed surprised.

"Why wouldn't I? It's easy as pie."

"Well, come on up and show the class."

"Be glad to."

And so, dressed in her smashing black patent Mary Janes, which Mrs. Plump had given her for her birthday, and her equally awesome white dress, Flor went up to the front of the class.

"I need a compass, a ruler, and a nice big marker," she said. "Now everybody pay attention. You think I'm just drawing spirals, but the truth is, spirals are all around you in the world. Spirals are in sunflowers and seashells, the inside of your ear, and galaxies . . . the magic is all around you, and math helps us describe it."

An hour later, she was in line for the more-popular-than-ever pie shop. Mrs. Plump and Dr. Pi had decided to go into business together. A new awning stretched over both shops: DR. PI AND MRS. PLUMP'S SKY-HIGH PIES,

TOAST, AND TEA—HALF THE BUTTER AND TWICE THE TASTE!

Mrs. Plump had become creative with her recipes. She now served swirly toast that went round and round and up and up and was stuffed with goodies like raisins and nuts. And Dr. Pi now catered to the diet set—you could order "diet" pie with three times the fruit and very little sugar.

"How *are* you, Edna?" asked Flor. "Love the yellow belt!"

"Yellow brings out the black of my dress," said Edna cheerfully. "I'll never abandon black, but a little color is acceptable now and then."

Dr. Pi was at his counter, bald and busy as ever. He gave Flor a warm smile when he saw her. "How are you?"

"I'm really happy!" she said.

"Ah." He nodded. "There is nothing truer than happiness, and nothing happier than the truth. Anyway, I'm in a rush. Could you bring pie over to the two gentlemen at the corner table?"

"Sure," she said cheerfully. "As long as you save a piece for me."

She couldn't decide who was more handsome today, Mr. Bit or Mr. It. With their wavy blond hair and white suits, they got a lot of attention. They had lingered here on Earth for weeks now, mainly because Mr. Bit was a 100 percent devotee of sky-high pie. He was the first customer waiting outside the door on Wednesday, and the last to leave.

Every time he saw Flor he broke into a big grin and shook her hand heartily.

"Hi, Mr. Bit, how's numbers?"

"Marvelous, miss. How's spirals?"

"Moving in the right direction."

"You blowing hot or cold today?"

"Not blowing either way. Just came here for pie."

"Oh my."

She raised an eyebrow. "Oh my? That's the best you can do? How about, this pie . . . is to die . . ."

"For," he finished.

She nodded.

"He's happy here," said Mr. It. "But one of these days we'll be on our way and go back to Planet Dog."

"One of these days," agreed Mr. Bit, suddenly morose.

"You belong with us! You should stick around," said Flor.

Mr. Bit brightened.

"You think so, miss?"

"For sure. I read it in a little book."

"A little book about the Bernoullis? What did it say?"

"It went something like this: 'The famous twins, Mr. Bit and Mr. It of Brooklyn Heights, New York, can be found every Wednesday at the Sky-High Pie, Toast, and Tea Shop. They wear white suits even in the middle of winter. If you wish to interview them, get in line. It will be a long, long line.'"

"A long, long line. Sounds mighty fine!" said Mr. Bit.

Flor sighed. Life couldn't be better.

And really, it would have been like any other wonderful Wednesday, except suddenly it wasn't. Because something really, really spooky happened. Right before their eyes, the pies changed. The beautiful Sky-High Pies started to droop. They drooped, and then they dropped, and then they flattened out.

"What's happening?" exclaimed Edna, across the shop. "My toast—my toast won't turn!"

Just then a howling wind blew the doors of the pie shop wide open, and they banged so hard the windows trembled.

It began to pour, a hard, driving gray rain like spears of steel ramming against the ground.

"My toast is turning back to squares!" Edna cried.

"All the pies have turned to rectangles," said Mr. It.

Flor looked at Dr. Pi, who had shut the doors to his shop and locked them against the wind.

Then she looked at Mr. Bit.

"One, two, three, four, one, two, three, four, nevermore and nevermore," he was repeating nervously.

"What's happening?" she whispered.

"It's rectangles, corners, angles, and lines!" he burst out. "One, two, three, four. Nevermore, and nevermore!"

"What does that mean?" she asked.

"Square Man." Mr. Bit looked very, very unhappy. "I met him once, when I was wandering among numbers. He goes through the universe destroying anything round.

Including spirals. I love a good rectangle, who wouldn't, who couldn't? But a world without circles, spirals, whorls, and whirls? Without curves and twirls? What kind of world is that?"

Just then they heard, ever so faintly, like a distant sonic boom, a voice: "One, two, three, four, nevermore and nevermore!"

"That's what he chants," said Mr. Bit, "while he does a square dance."

"He's the true enemy of the Spiral," said Dr. Pi. "And it looks like he has finally found me."

ACKNOWLEDGMENTS

My deepest appreciation for thoughtful readings to Cathy Altman-Nocquet and her daughter Sarah, Sue Mingus and her grandniece Emma, Tyler Volk, and Paul Shemin. Thanks to Emily Lawrence for being a wonderful editor, and to Edward Necarsulmer IV, a literary agent matched by none.

Read on for an exciting sneak peek
at Flor's next adventure!

THE GOLDEN RECTANGLE

Gillian Neimark

THE PIE SHOP CALAMITY

Flor opened her closet door and reached up to the top shelf. There it was. Just where she'd put it months ago. The magic book. She sat down on the bed, her hands moving slowly over a soft, peeling calfskin cover. The title of the book was long: *The History of the Bernoulli Family from the Seventeenth Century Until Present Times*. It not only told the story of her famous ancestors in Switzerland and France, but it actually recorded events as they happened. The print just appeared on the blank pages. "Present Times" really meant present times.

She'd taped her magic key to the inside cover, and she pulled off the tape now, holding the key in her palm. It looked like the key to an ancient castle door. She turned it over, saying aloud the words engraved on it:

"*Eadem mutata resurgo semperdem.*"

And then she translated the saying. "I shall arise again the same, though changed. Always."

Those were the words that one of her ancestors, Jakob Bernoulli, had carved on his gravestone. It was a saying about the Spiral. The Spiral could be found in everything from seashells to galaxies.

Dr. Pi had explained the saying on the key this way: "The Spiral is unique because it gets bigger and bigger without changing its shape at all. Do you know anything else that can do that? And we are all like that Spiral. Though we change and grow and learn through life, something deep in us remains the same."

Life had certainly changed her. And it looked like life was about to change her again. And yet Dr. Pi was right—she was still the same Flor Bernoulli, a ten-year-old Brooklyn girl whose dream was to be a fashion designer.

"Dr. Pi told me to look in the book, and I'd know what to do," she said aloud now. "So let's see what clues my future holds."

She pasted the key back into the book and opened to the last chapter. It had been a while since she'd looked in the magic book, and she had some catching up to do.

"There is a cosmic fire of life," she read. "And it moves and brings alive all the things of this universe. Stars and trees, butterflies and flowers, birds and lions and tigers and grasshoppers and humans, rivers and mountains, everything alive has a fire within. Flor Bernoulli learned how to channel this fire. She followed the directions written on a scroll that was hidden in a magic key and was able to bring a dead man back to life."

Flor looked up. Yes, the book was right. She had breathed life into Mr. Bit after he died, and he had come alive again. Her heart was beating so fast. Did she really want to know the rest? She looked down and began to read once more.

"Dr. Pi was guardian of the Secret Spiral, and for centuries it was safe under his careful watch. But out in the far reaches of the universe, his enemy planned the day he would destroy Dr. Pi, and destroy every last spiral that existed. His name was Square Man. He was made of nothing but squares. His eyes, his hands, his legs, even the heart that beat inside him, all were square."

She shivered. Square Man sounded truly creepy. She went on reading.

"Square Man had great power, though he had not come by that power honestly. He had stolen it. Once upon a time there was a place known as the Beginning of all Beginnings. Therein were points. And the points multiplied, and fell all in a row like beads on a wire. And they became lines. And the lines flowed forward. Some lines curved. They curved until they met themselves again and became circles. Some lines stopped at a length they liked, and met up with other lines and joined together. They became triangles, or rectangles, or squares, or five- and six-pointed stars. Some lines became beautiful golden rectangles. Golden rectangles gave birth to forever-curving lines known as spirals.

"Then the shapes went forth and multiplied on planets everywhere. But on one planet, in one house, in one room, something went wrong. It was a lovely planet, round as a glowing glass globe, and everyone in it was soft and curved and cuddly. But then a little boy was born, and he was not round at all. He was square. He was a square that had lost its way. He should have gone to a planet like Earth, where every shape is welcome. Or he could have gone to a planet of rectangles. But he went to a round planet. And they did not want him. They found him very amusing. They laughed and laughed whenever they saw him. They thought he was so funny-looking. Finally they sent him back to the Beginning of all Beginnings, with a note that he should be delivered elsewhere, to a place where he fit in. But when he arrived there, nobody could decide where to send him. The points argued and argued. And while they were arguing, Square Man saw a beautiful line lying on the floor. He could not quite say why it seemed so beautiful to him. He picked it up. And while they were arguing, he left. He had stolen a very powerful wand. It could pull a circle apart and turn it back into a line. It could take a spiral and unwind it into a rectangle. It could take a line and explode it back into points. Once he learned what the wand could do, he was unstoppable. And he decided he did not want to be sent to another planet. He did not ever want to be laughed at again. 'I will turn the entire universe into squares with this special wand,' he said to himself. 'And I'll start with that planet over there. That will be my home. I will call it Planet Square.'"

Just then Flor's mother knocked on her door. Hastily Flor shoved the book under her pillow and lay down, pulling her quilt up around her shoulders. Her mother opened the door.

Flor rubbed her eyes and said sleepily, "I know, I'm grounded."

Her mother nodded, satisfied.

"I'll see you tomorrow, darling. I'm going to watch some old movies on television."

Flor yawned.

Her mother shut the door, and Flor listened as her mom walked down the long hallway of their railroad apartment, to the living room at the other end. Then she quickly pulled the book out. But she skipped ahead to the final page, where the last paragraph read:

"When Square Man first arrived on planet Earth, he

decided to give Dr. Pi a special greeting. Nobody saw him walk into the bakery, because he was so small. He just trotted in behind an older, married couple. And he sat in the corner watching the hustle and bustle. He listened to the customers 'ooh' and 'aah' over the spiral pies. He heard them moan and groan with delight when they tasted the buttery crust and warm fruit filling. He held his magic wand, ready for the right moment. And the right moment came just when Flor sat down to eat. Holding a small knob on the wand, he wound it like a fishing reel. He pointed it at one pie after another, winding the knob, as if he were reeling in a fish. He was unwinding the spirals. And all the pies went flat and turned into rectangles. Then he unwound the spiral toast. And then, still sitting in the corner, he laughed out loud, as he chanted his anthem and watched the customers run from the store. Dr. Pi didn't even see him as he left.

"'I'll be back,' he proclaimed, though nobody heard. 'But first I need to check out this golden rectangle of hay. So it's off to Puddleville for a day.'"

"Puddleville?" said Flor out loud. "Where the heck is that?"

Just then there was a tap at the window. Flor went over and was astonished to see that Dr. Pi had arrived on her fire escape.

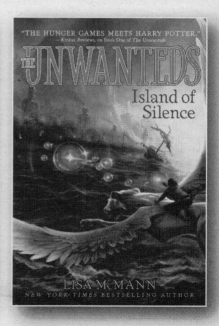

BE SURE TO CATCH
FABLEHAVEN

Available from Aladdin

FROM ALADDIN · PUBLISHED BY SIMON & SCHUSTER

"Do I have family in the Imagine Nation?" Jack asked. "Are they superheroes?"

"You're a mystery, Jack. But that's all about to change."

Don't miss the thrilling adventures of Jack Blank, who could be either the savior of the Imagine Nation and the world beyond, or the biggest threat they've ever faced. And even Jack himself doesn't know which it will be. . . .

EBOOK EDITIONS ALSO AVAILABLE

Can one girl make eleven
wishes come true?

THE
Wish
Stealers

TRACY TRIVAS

NOW AVAILABLE IN
PAPERBACK

FROM ALADDIN ✳ PUBLISHED BY SIMON & SCHUSTER